POPCORN AND PANIC

THE PERIDALE CAFE SERIES - BOOK 24

AGATHA FROST

About This Book

Released: *September 13th 2022*
Words: *58,000*
Series: *Book 24 - Peridale Cozy Café Mystery Series*
Standalone: *Yes*
Cliff-hanger: *No*

When Julia's full-time café return clashes with a festival, thousands of music lovers descending on the village should be precisely what she needs to kick off a new era. But the council throws a spanner in the works when her cafe is "required not to operate" due to blocked road access. The front entrance, that is, and with the festival happening right behind her café, the kernels of a plan begin to pop...

And it seems like the perfect plan to get through the hectic weekend until the lead singer of the headlining band, Electric Fury, dies before he gets a chance to perform on the main stage. Having witnessed how the victim, Jett Fury, interacted with his entourage, Julia is sure there's more to the story than the local Detective Inspector's "accidental" theory.

While picking up the pieces after the destructive

weekend, Julia hears the beat of a different song. From the rockstar's secretive wife to his new drummer, unscrupulous agent, and even an obsessed groupie, many have something to gain from Jett's death. Can Julia pluck through the lies chorded around the rockstar's life and strike the right note to uncover Jett Fury's killer?

WANT TO BE KEPT UP TO DATE WITH AGATHA FROST RELEASES? *SIGN UP THE FREE NEWSLETTER!*

www.AgathaFrost.com

You can also follow **Agatha Frost** across social media. Search 'Agatha Frost' on:

Facebook
Twitter
Goodreads
Instagram

ALSO BY AGATHA FROST

Other

*J*ulia South-Brown held her breath as she added another tentative drop of pink food colouring to the bowl while heavy rock music bellowed around her cottage's small kitchen.

Folding in the bright streaks, she glanced at the radio on top of the fridge. Had she slipped the station dial after Mowgli's attempt to knock it off the counter? Trying to tune out the electric guitar's screeching in her ear, she hoped she hadn't sent the buttercream too far towards the lurid magenta of her first attempt. The unappetising hue wasn't stopping Mowgli from licking at the abandoned bowl on the edge of the breakfast bar, and a dunk of her finger confirmed that it was the perfect combination of rich and sweet.

She hadn't been able to resist starting over.

As experienced as a baker as she was, she wouldn't call herself a total perfectionist regarding her creations. Taste always triumphed. However, the vision for this particular cake had been circling for a while. She'd been excited to start, assuming she still had months for at least one practice round of the special bake. After Katie's surprise invitation that morning, she'd only had a few hours and lots of hope to bring that vision to life.

Did it need another drop?

A glance at the cat clock with its swishing eyes and tail let her know she'd be late if she dared to test that theory. The rock band on the radio reached a dizzying crescendo of guitars and drums, all while a man wailed in falsetto. She slathered the buttercream onto the stacked base of four sponge cakes to stop her tinkering. Whatever the song was, the wild crowd loved it.

Checking the dial, she was surprised to see she was listening to the same local station with the breezy pop music that never failed to have Olivia bouncing in her highchair over breakfast. Maybe the Sunday schedule was for a different crowd. Good thing Olivia wasn't there; her teething crying had been enough to cause headaches without the loud music unnecessarily setting her off.

Julia flicked off the radio and began smoothing out the buttercream with a sigh of relief. A few careful rotations, helped along with her expert light touch and the late-summer heat, had the baby pink surface as smooth as glass. In the quiet, it didn't take long for Olivia's gurgles to drift in from the direction of the front garden. Julia smiled, picking up the cake's second tier, already wrapped in a smooth layer of black marzipan.

Holding her breath again, she placed the thinner black level onto the buttercream. Resisting the urge to pull out a ruler to make sure it was in the centre – so maybe a *little* bit of a perfectionist – she grabbed the piping bag. Twisting the black icing to the thin tip, she hovered over an oval of white marzipan.

Noon was ticking closer.

No time to overthink.

'Congratulations, Katie!'

Julia pressed the edible label to the smooth pink surface with a little sugar glaze and a silent prayer. In an ideal world, she'd have had time to wait for the buttercream to dry to a frosty crust, but on such a warm day, that would take until sunset. She carefully pulled her fingers away and waited for the whole thing to fall apart. When it didn't, she slid it from the turntable into her tallest cake box, and with only minutes to spare to set off to Mulberry

Lane in time, she snatched up her keys and hurried for the door.

Reclining in a deckchair, her husband, Barker, looked over his reading glasses from behind his folded paperback – a crime thriller, no doubt. "And here I thought I'd had an impressive morning reading a hundred pages. What do you think of Mummy's cake, Olivia?"

Their daughter splashed her fists in the paddling pool by Barker's feet in the shade of an oak tree. She couldn't have looked more adorable in her shades and summer hat. A string of vowels that almost resembled words babbled out, and her smile that showed her first two bottom teeth was as bright as the sunshine.

"Quite the review." With the cake box hugged to her chest, Julia hurried to the gate as fast as she dared. "You'll both need a sunscreen top up in half an hour, and there are teething rings in the freezer."

"I'll chomp on them with glee," Barker said with a smile. "Have you heard about this music festival everyone's talking about online?"

"Think I might have heard one of the bands playing on the radio."

"But it hasn't happened yet."

"I shouldn't be too long." Her hip pushed open the gate as she waved with a daring hand. "You can tell me all about it when we get back to our regularly scheduled lazy Sunday."

She strapped the cake behind the seatbelt in the passenger seat of her beloved vintage Ford Anglia, its aqua blue exterior a perfect complement to the pink buttercream. She slammed the door, another flash of aqua blue catching her eye from the top of the winding lane. A teenage girl was walking towards her, her creamy blue hair hanging from underneath a black hoodie. She was hauling a backpack almost her size, and Julia's stomach flipped.

Just for a moment, she thought she saw her adopted daughter, Jessie, but the girl grew younger with every step closer. Silly, considering Jessie was eight hours ahead and six thousand miles east.

"This Peridale?"

"Last time I checked."

The girl rolled her eyes and carried on walking, hunched over from the bag. She looked back over her shoulder and barked, "B&B?"

"Straight down, right at the village green. You can't miss..."

The girl with the blue hair continued on without so much as a 'thank you', but Julia had other things to do. Before she got caught behind the fleet of lorries trundling from the same direction, she set off towards

Mulberry Lane, bubbling with excitement over what she was about to see.

2

$\mathcal{W}$ith one hand on the wheel, and the other forcing the cake box into the seat, Julia bounced down the cobbled road of Peridale's centuries-old shopping street. Among the crooked walls of golden Cotswold stone and jauntily angled roofs, one shop stood out from the rest. Nestled between a florist and a baby clothes boutique, its freshly sandblasted brick exterior wasn't even its most notable feature. Julia was impressed that she could see the glowing neon pink sign of the nail salon, considering the time of day, yet it shone like her first buttercream attempt.

Given Katie's turbulent year, Julia could hardly believe she was looking at a shop with her stepmother's name glowing above the door.

"You weren't lying when you said it was finished," Julia said as she let herself into the shop. "How?"

"Incredible, isn't it?" As she rushed to greet Julia at the door, Katie's feet bounced like a giddy toddler. "Is this for me?"

"Unless you know someone else who'd want a giant nail varnish bottle cake?"

Julia slid the plastic box onto an acrylic reception desk filled with neon tubes as blinding as the sign. Pink had always been Katie's signature colour. However, she'd shown more restraint throughout the rest of the salon, opting for the softer powdered blush shade Julia had been painstakingly trying to colour match in the icing. During one of their café shifts last week, Katie had casually mentioned the name of the paint, and it looked even prettier in person. She plucked off the lid, and though the oval label had slid down a little, the colour wasn't far off.

"I've never seen anything like it." Katie's plump-lipped smile grew as tears swelled amongst her coated bottom lashes. "You didn't have to."

"Didn't I?" Julia accepted Katie's tight-squeezing hug. "If you hadn't been running my café, I wouldn't have had so much time at home with Olivia this year. It's the *least* I could do."

"After everything *I've* done?" Katie let out one of her girlish giggles as she carefully dabbed at her tears.

"I couldn't have done *any* of this if you hadn't given me a chance to spread my business wings. No offence to your father, but he knows more about hunting antiques than running a business, and modelling hardly had transferable skills." She bit into her wobbly smile. "So, do you like it?"

"I *love* it, Katie." Julia laughed, taking in the fluffy white pillows on the pink leather sofa in the waiting area to the glimmering crystal chandelier to the wall holding an endless rainbow of organised polishes. "I'm just shocked that it's finished. It was a white box when I came last week. Forget that. It was a burnt-out shell of a bookshop when you bought the place. How did you pull this off? I thought you wouldn't be ready until closer to Christmas?"

"Who's ever heard of a building project being finished *ahead* of time?" Katie joined Julia in taking in the transformation. "Once they put in the new electrics last week, it's just been a matter of painting and putting in all the stuff I've been buying since the manor sold. Before I realised it, your father and I were standing here last night, and it was finished. Do you honestly love it?"

"It's perfect." Julia walked over to the wall of polish. "It's you. It's all you."

"Now, pick a shade. You're going to be my first official customer. On the house, of course."

Honoured, Julia selected the shade closest to the buttercream, and Katie wasted no time. The days of buffing Julia's skin and smashing her cuticles with torture tools were long gone, and Katie had framed her qualifications certificates to prove it. She'd become a decent baker over her time at the café, but for the first time in the years Julia had known Katie, she seemed to be genuinely in her element.

"When's the grand opening?"

"As soon as the insurance is sorted," she said, shaking up the polish after preparing Julia's nails. "I haven't quite figured out how to juggle it with the café, but I will. Maybe I'll only open nights, just until Jessie gets back. Is she still home for Christmas?"

"As far as I know." Julia squirmed in her seat. "Katie, you can't run both."

"I'll manage while you're still taking maternity leave." Katie's head lowered as the first coat went on. "That's not why I asked you here, Julia. I promised I'd work until Jessie came home from her travelling, and that's exactly what I'll do. I won't let you down."

"Katie, you—"

"No, Julia." Katie tried to hide the yawn fluttering her lips. "After all those years at the manor worrying about what designer shoes went with what handbag, I don't have a right to complain about working. I want to set a better example for my

Vinnie than my father set for me. Like I said, I'll manage."

"It might be a *slight* overcorrection."

Julia glanced back at the cake, and even though she'd felt rushed through it, she'd still spent the morning, and many days like it, at home with Olivia. Katie's thick concealer couldn't hide the exhaustion Julia knew all too well after her years working at the café. Like full-time motherhood, days in the café could range from relaxing to exhausting – most a combination of the two, depending on the hour. As if running the village's only café wasn't enough, Katie had been cramming in nail clients on the side while rescuing Trotter's Books from its scorched state. This wasn't why Julia had offered Katie the job, and her part-time shifts were only easing the burden a little.

Julia knew what she had to do.

She wasn't sure if she was ready to go back full-time.

Would she ever be?

"Katie..." Julia gulped down her doubts. "My café shouldn't have to fit into that juggling act."

"How can I leave you to run it by yourself?"

"How can *I* leave *you* to do the same?"

Katie fought for a response, but none came. Glancing up through her lashes, she said, "You're right. It'll probably be too much."

"Most definitely."

"I never had to quit modelling. The phone just stopped ringing. Do I have to write you a letter?"

"Let's not bother with the technicalities." Julia winked, blowing on the nails of her finished hand. "Effective as of *immediately*, you're relieved of your duties because you have *your* dream to chase, and it's time I got back to mine. Now, should we try this cake before it melts in the—"

Julia turned around as the marzipan label slid off the edge of her morning's effort. It splattered onto the sparkly white tiles, dragging away the buttercream to reveal the sponges underneath, taking the nail varnish bottle illusion with it.

"Oh, dear. Do you believe in omens?"

"No." Julia pulled two plates, two forks, and a knife from her handbag. "But I do believe in these September heatwaves we keep getting. Now, do you want to eat the bottle or cap?"

3

*J*ulia sprang out of bed the next day as exuberantly as she had on her café's opening morning over six years ago. She'd worked out how long it had been while falling asleep to the sound of Barker's soft snoring the night before. Four and a half years since she'd run the place on her own too, and it wasn't a coincidence that was when Jessie, then a homeless sixteen-year-old, crashed into her life. She'd worked that out in Jessie's old bedroom, now Olivia's nursery, after being woken up by the teething cries in the dead of night.

"You should probably eat something." Barker took the spoonful of porridge from her as she fed Olivia at the breakfast bar. "Big day ahead."

She let out a shaky stream of air through pursed

lips, picking up the wholegrain slice she'd only taken a single bite from. "I know it's not my *first* first day, but it's like my nerves don't know the difference."

"You could always close for a week or two? It would give you time to advertise and find someone, so you're not alone. Or I could come and help?"

"And your clients?"

"What clients?" Barker flew the spoon into Olivia's mouth like an aeroplane. "Four phone calls, three emails, two meetings, and still, Barker Brown, PI hasn't taken on a single new case all month."

"Then we definitely can't afford for me to close the café." Julia pushed the toast away and took in a mouthful of coffee, but that didn't sit right in her stomach either. "I'm as excited as I am nervous, which makes no sense because I've been at the café, but..."

Julia wasn't sure what she was trying to say, and the radio wasn't helping. They were playing that same song that had almost given her a headache while finishing the nail varnish cake.

Lightning in a bottle.
Girl, you go full throttle.
Making my heart blow up.
Every time you show up.
Lightning in a bottle...

"You don't want to be late on your not-first-day-but-feels-like-your-first-day day." He placed the strap of her handbag over her shoulder and gave her back a comforting rub. "Well, you could be. You could shorten the hours and shave off whole days if you wanted to. Just remember that it's your name above the door. You don't have to figure it all out right now. One day at a time."

"One day at a time."

"You're in control."

"I'm in control." She gave Olivia a kiss and a cuddle before letting herself slip off the breakfast bar stool. "I should make a quick exit before she realises it's Monday and I'm not staying. If you need anything, if anything goes wrong—"

"I'll know exactly what to do." He lifted Olivia out of her highchair. "Don't worry. It's just a quiet Monday in Peridale. What could go wrong?"

"Did you have to say that?"

"*Nothing* will go wrong." He slid on a pair of black sunglasses and pulled open the back door. "Now then, would Madam care for a splash in the paddling pool before the summer leaves us behind?"

Despite suggesting a quick exit, Julia wanted nothing more than to follow them into the garden as the morning warmed up after its chilly start. She'd known the maternity bubble couldn't last forever. As her gran kept reminding her, she had a life and a business before the baby came along. But the familiar guilt that fizzed up whenever she knew she wouldn't be spending the whole day with her daughter took over.

There was something else peppering the edges.

Guilt at *wanting* to leave, to see who she was, alone in her café after so many years and changes. And that only made her feel more guilty about the fact she was leaving.

Her mind was racing, and the radio wasn't helping.

"That was 'Lightning in a Bottle' by Electric Fury," the chipper DJ announced over the fading outro of the crowd-infused song, "who you can see performing live *this* weekend at the Cotswold Crowd..."

Julia flicked off the radio, glad of the peace. She tickled Mowgli's smoky grey fur as he brushed his whiskers against the fridge with a soft purr.

"I'm leaving you in charge," she whispered. "Be good."

In the hallway, she slipped into her trusty burgundy Oxfords with black laces, a treat to herself to celebrate her part-time return earlier that summer. After one last look down the hallway, glad to hear

Olivia's laughter rather than tears, Julia flattened out the creases in her pale-yellow summer dress and closed the cottage door.

"One day at a time."

No idea what the day alone in the café would bring, her excitement bubbled into a smile that banished the nerves long enough to get her into the car.

With the gleaming kitchen behind her two hours later, Julia clutched the beaded curtain separating her workspace from the inviting pastels of the café. Behind the counter, the latte cups and porcelain mugs were so neat it seemed a shame to disturb them. Cakes of all kinds twirled under spotlights as they waited to be sliced in the tall display case. The less dazzlingly lit cabinet in front of the coffee machine was stuffed full of scones and cupcakes, which Julia would have to restock if there was a lunchtime rush.

Starting at the counter, a string of postcards from Jessie's globe-trotting filled the longest wall. The opposite wall had tasteful black and white photographs of Peridale and its countryside. Beyond the rows of precisely positioned tables filled with menus and stuffed sugar pots, the sun dazzled through the freshly polished windows in warm speckled lines. Seeing the café in its perfect state should have eased Julia, but the knot of nerves only grew the closer she came to opening time. Running the café alone would be just as she remembered, or so she hoped.

Those early days alone felt so long ago.

A divorce ago.

An adoption ago.

A marriage ago.

A baby ago.

But there was no time to think about that.

Naturally, her grandmother, Dot, was at the door five minutes before opening. From the jiggle of her shoulders, her foot was tapping on the step. Behind her were her husband, Percy, and Evelyn, the owner of the local B&B.

"Where's Katie? I didn't think you worked Mondays."

"Change of plan, Gran. I'm back."

"You're back?" Dot arched a brow. "As in *back* back?"

"*Back* back."

"Well, thank goodness for that! The dear tried her best, but nobody can make a cake like you."

"Katie brought her bubbly energy to the place,"

Evelyn countered, hugging Julia. "Has it been a year already?"

"Almost!"

"Oh, it's good to have you back."

"And she was quite good at giving advice," added Percy, "in her funny way."

"She's certainly left her mark," Julia said, returning to the counter to start on their orders, which she knew from memory. "She reorganised the mugs and cups, so they're easier to reach, and her way of stacking the fridge is much better for space."

"Cakes aside," said Dot as she took her seat at the head of the large table she'd rearranged, "I didn't think she had the stones to keep up with it all, so I'm happy to report that she royally proved me wrong."

"And I do love how she's redrawn the menu," Evelyn pointed out with a swish of her bright orange kaftan. "The little illustrations of the cakes are rather lovely."

"Where's Shilpa?" Dot thought aloud, distracted by her watch. "And Amy. And Johnny, for that matter."

"This isn't an *official* Peridale's Ears meeting, my love," Percy pointed out. "We did say it was *just* breakfast."

"Well, since many of us are here, I'm calling this an official meeting." Dot split the folder with a slap of leather on the table. She clicked her pen and started,

"Following the mighty success of our recent charity clothing drive, I've arranged for us to undertake a food drive to help the local..."

Before Dot sucked Julia away from the café and into another of her neighbourhood watch meetings, Julia returned to work. Dot could no longer insist Katie was doing fine on her own as an excuse for dragging Julia into conversations that could loop around in the same cycles for endless hours.

One advantage of working alone.

While she cut each of them a slice of Victoria sponge cake to celebrate the change, the bell above the door announced Shilpa's arrival from the post office next door.

"You're late," Dot said without looking up from her folder.

"Do forgive me for conversing with one of my customers." Shilpa waved a greeting to Julia before sitting down. "I thought this was *just* breakfast?"

"It's never *just* breakfast when there's a whole village to keep in order," she said, glancing at Julia as though wondering where their free slices of cake were. "Have you heard about this music festival that's apparently coming to Peridale this weekend?"

The post dropped onto the doormat, and her gran had hold of it before Julia could get out from behind the counter. She flicked through the stack, abandoning the letters on a table after plucking out a shiny photograph card.

"Would you look at that? A new postcard from Jessie!"

Julia's chest fluttered as Dot wafted the card, tempting Julia over to what had become the neighbourhood watch corner. She ducked to see the picture on the postcard. She saw a tower that looked like a modernised Eiffel – or Blackpool – tower. Unlike those, this red and white structure jutted from a dense cityscape, set against a snow-peaked mountain and a clear blue sky.

"Hm. Japan." Dot turned the card to look at the picture again. "She couldn't be further from home if she tried."

Julia held out her hand to no avail.

"I think New Zealand might be the furthest place from us," said Evelyn, and Dot's lips puckered at the correction. "But how I *adore* Japan. It's been so long since I've been so far east. Such a spiritual, cultural place, and the people couldn't be more polite."

"How long has it been now?" asked Percy.

"Feels like only yesterday that she left," said Shilpa.

If only it felt like yesterday for Julia.

"Nine months."

The all-too-familiar pining whisked into a froth in

her chest. She didn't want the feeling to take root, especially when she had so much to sort out. Jessie was, after all, having the time of her life, and every new postcard added to the string moved them closer to their reunion. But still, her heart ached, each new card a reminder of how long it had been since she'd last hugged her eldest daughter.

"Gran..." Julia flapped her hand again, and Dot finally relinquished the postcard. She quickly read over it. Jessie's scrawly handwriting was always a comfort, as illegible as it sometimes was. "They missed cherry blossom season, but they've been having fun in karaoke bars, they've been to a train station run by cats, and the city is the cleanest they've been to. She's eaten sushi every day, and they were heading to a temple on the afternoon she wrote this. She misses everyone and can't wait to see us all soon."

Julia treasured the postcards the most, if only to see Jessie's handwriting, and her customers loved following along. She walked around the counter and clipped the postcard under the next wooden peg on the string under the 'Jessie's Travels' sign.

"This alleged festival?" Dot pushed. "Have you heard anything about it, Julia?"

"Barker mentioned something about a festival yesterday morning."

"There's no *alleged* about it." Shilpa accepted her

latte from Julia with a gracious smile. "That's why I was late. I was talking to a young lady who works at the police station."

"Oh?" Dot sat upright.

"She was changing her Euros back to Stirling, and I wouldn't ask why, but I'd only converted the same money for her last week, and she seemed so excited for her cruise." She paused to sip her latte, and Dot moved in closer. "She said she'd had to cancel because *every* officer is needed to work during a festival this weekend."

"Such short notice?" said Julia.

"This morning's tea leaves were rather difficult to decipher," said Evelyn, clutching her crystals, "But now that I'm thinking about it, they did look like musical notes. How I adore festivals."

"I'm *sure* they did." Dot rolled her eyes. "What are we going to do about this? We need to protest. We *must*!"

"Why would you want to protest a festival?" Percy fiddled with his round red spectacles as Julia slid the cake slices from the tray onto the table. "Unless you're joking?"

"That blasted Ethel White and her Peridale's Eyes will only beat us to the punch."

"I heard she was a little light on members these days," he said. "And festivals are supposed to be fun, my love."

"I'm with Percy on that one, Gran."

"Festivals attract people in *droves*, Julia. *Droves!*"

"I can't imagine why," Shilpa muttered. "Julia and Percy are right. It could be a good time, depending on who is on the line-up. Don't you remember *fun*, Dorothy? It doesn't always have to be binocular watches and logistic meetings."

"People bring *trouble*." Dot's voice rose as though she couldn't believe they weren't all seeing her point of view. "Think of the noise. Think of the *litter*! This village's *leading* neighbourhood watch team must do something about this." She wagged a finger in the air, and Julia sensed a declaration on the way. "Mark my words. A festival big enough to have the local constabulary scrambling to ground their officers will be a disaster."

Not in the mood to dissuade her gran from causing trouble in the name of village peace, Julia took the rest of the letters into the kitchen, glad she hadn't been rushed off her feet just yet. She flicked through the post.

A water bill.

A flyer promising faster internet.

And a letter from the council.

Julia ripped open the latter, and the contents were

brief enough that her heart dropped to the pit of her stomach after only a few seconds of reading:

Dear Mrs South-Brown,

*Your business, **Julia's Café**, will be required not to operate from Thursday 3rd – Monday 7th per health and safety protocol 73b. This is due to a lack of road access to the front of your business owing to its proximity to the rear entrance of the planned **Cotswold Crowd Pleaser Festival** that is taking place in Peridale village from Friday 4th – Sunday 6th. We apologise for the inconvenience, and as a courtesy for the short notice, 50% of your average income will be provided, details of which can be found on Page 2. If you have any questions, do not hesitate to contact us using the details below.*

Yours sincerely,

Cotswold Council – Road and Planning Department

.   .   .

"Only me." Her father's voice from the direction of the back door broke her away from reading the letter for the third time. "Just wanted to pop by and personally thank you for the chance you gave Katie. You've been such a guiding light for her, so this is just a small token of my appreciation."

Julia looked at the bouquet of sunflowers in her father's hands, but she couldn't bring herself to smile. He read the letter over her shoulder.

"I can't believe it. Fifty percent? It's an outrage!" Brian's roar brought Dot to the beads immediately. "Have you seen this, Mother? The council are trying to swindle Julia."

Dot snatched the letter and inhaled its contents in a moment.

"I told you this would bring trouble!" she cried, slapping it down. "We *are* protesting. How can they do this at such short notice?"

"An old music producer friend called last night about this festival. Think he wanted somewhere to stay, but I didn't have the heart to tell him we'd sold the manor." Brian leaned in. "Said the original location was sold at auction, only nobody told the organisers. Quite the scandal."

"And in steps our high and mighty council to save the day and ruin our village in the process." Dot was pacing around the island. "Forget fifty percent. As much as I'd rather watch paint dry than attend, a festival in the village would have this place full *every* second of *every* day. They owe you five *hundred* percent! They simply cannot do this to you."

Julia wished she hadn't wasted so much energy worrying about her first day back that morning. "They can and are."

"Bull to that." Brian dumped the sunflowers in the sink and went for the back door. "They only said front entrance. You can just let people in through the back. Easy. What do you think, Mum?"

"I think that's an easy way of getting Julia in trouble, but when don't your schemes end in disaster?" Foot tapping, Dot stared off into the corner of the room. "There *must* be another way around this."

The three of them sat in silence for a moment, but Julia wasn't thinking about a way to fix things. As excited as she'd been for her big comeback, she couldn't shake the slight relief washing over her.

"I don't believe it," Dot said from the doorstep, shielding her eyes from the sun. "They've already started putting up the stage. *Percy!*" she bellowed over her shoulder. "Fetch my megaphone and gather the troops. We have a festival to stop."

Julia joined her gran on the doorstep. At the far end of the field that stretched out behind the café, the beginnings of a metal structure glittered in the distance. Even if her gran led the charge, Julia didn't have the energy to fight the slow-moving council with so little time to go.

"I don't think you're going to stop the festival."

"Well, what *are* we going to do?"

"I wouldn't be able to keep up with how busy it would be on my own anyway," she said with a sigh. "Maybe it's for the best. Gives me more time to figure something out." Still on the doorstep, staring out at the never-ending field, Julia could already see it full of potential customers she had no access to. Or maybe she did? "What if they don't come *into* the café?"

"That's *it*!" her father's fingers snapped together. "I think I have just the thing."

"No schemes, Brian."

"It's not a scheme, Mother. It's a business opportunity."

Julia almost refused. As well-intentioned as he was, her father's attempts to problem solve often resulted in worse situations. She could return to the bubble of the cottage, and maybe even attend the festival as a guest. Remembering Barker's lack of clients, as her gran had pointed out, she was about to miss out on the busiest weekend the village might ever have. The money would be tight, but fifty percent was better than nothing.

The glint in her father's eye intrigued her enough to lean in closer.

"What kind of opportunity?"

After a day of creeping festival fever in the café, Julia followed her father to a dark corner of his antique barn at the bottom of Mulberry Lane. She wafted away a cloud of dust after he pulled a paint-splattered sheet from a slender machine.

"Ta-da!"

Julia ran her fingers against its cold metal frame as the dust settled around them. Even without windows in the shop, the scuffed red chrome glinted like rubies in the parts that hadn't chipped away. She opened the door to the smoked glass cabinet and was hit with a scent of sweet and salty burnt butter that transported her to a cinema foyer. Like the corners of the scratched glass, the hanging metal kettle and bottom were blackened by time. Even without all the damage, the clunky black plug hinted it might have been as old as her father.

"Does it even still work?"

"Last time I checked." He gave it a gentle pat. "Never been able to sell the thing, but perhaps it was waiting for its moment to shine. Needs a clean-up, that's all. So, what do you think?"

"I think you might be onto something."

"Then leave it with me," he said with a wink. "Your old Dad has got this one sorted."

4

Over the next two days, before Julia was 'required not to operate', the well-oiled gossip channels spread the word of the Cotswold Crowd Pleaser's location change to every corner. Her full-time return was a footnote in the café's conversation, which had always been a meeting place to discuss the village's goings-on.

As with any topic, there was no clear consensus.

From what Julia gathered as she tried her best to keep up with the jangling bell above the door, people were pouring themselves into one of two cups in even measure. Half were fizzing with excitement for the village first, but it was the inhabitants planning to lock themselves in their cottages until the festival was over who were the most vocal.

"The *noise!*"

"What were they thinking?"

"The *litter!*"

"The council should have consulted us."

"The *vandalism!*"

"We simply do not have the space."

Despite Dot's best efforts as she helped with table clearing and washing up in the busiest hours, the complaints didn't rouse enough residents to protest.

On Wednesday night, as the first metal barriers went up around the village green, Julia was starting to wonder if the council had done her a favour. Keeping up with the locals was one thing, but if the rumours were to be believed, the festival usually attracted upwards of 'at least ten thousand people' over the weekend.

On Thursday morning, she clicked her phone to silent before anything else, intending to do nothing but rest. Lounging around the garden with Barker and Olivia, the familiar homelife routine was a delight to keep up with compared to the café.

"I know us Brits like to queue, but you should see this *monstrosity!*" Dot cried down the landline phone shortly after Julia had read Olivia to sleep. Julia was impressed her gran had shown such restraint by waiting so late in the day to call. "It looks like the waiting room to *hell!*"

As prone to exaggeration as her grandmother was, Julia couldn't think of a more apt description as she snaked through the structure constructed on the village green the following day. Not that there was much green left on display. The shoes of hundreds clunked against interconnected mats covering the grass, not too dissimilar from the foam playmats in Olivia's nursery. However, those were a soft grey, not the well-worn blood-red plastic shining up at Julia under the baking sun.

After fifteen minutes of shuffling around the metal maze, inching closer to the swelling bass sweeping in from the far end of the field, Julia reached the security checks and handed over her ticket. She gave herself up for a barely-there frisk from one security guard while another attached a plastic band around her wrist. The metal turnstile spat her out at the opening of the alley between the café and the post office.

Excited people of all ages rushed around her and past the place her car would have been parked if the week was like any other. She hadn't recognised any locals among the faces covered in glitter and neon paint dots. Not in the same rush to sprint to the field, she stared at the front of her café behind the metal cage. She wasn't sure she'd ever witnessed it in such a sorry state, but at least it was protected. As early in the day as it was, the village gossips might not have been fluffing the attendance numbers.

"*Julia!*" Her father's voice bellowed down the alley. "What are the odds? Looks like we had the same idea."

Brian tugged at the wide-open collar of a bright red shirt, its hue almost identical to the red vintage dress Julia had steamed before bed. She glanced at her café one last time before the stream carried her into the sea of people. She'd stared out to the field after many busy days, only seeing the odd dog walker here and there, but she'd never seen anything like this.

The sun shone from behind the monolith-like stage looming far off in the distance. The first act had yet to make an appearance. Still, thousands were milling around the field, pumping electricity into the atmosphere with their laughter and cheer. Long lines already stretched at a row of food trucks and bar tents, and the scent of hot dogs, fried onions, and beer was thick on the warm breeze.

"A bit of competition won't hurt," he said, meeting Julia before she reached the opening of the alley. He stood behind her and covered her eyes with his fingers. "Indulge your old dad for a minute."

Brian led her a short distance and positioned her on the cobbled path that ran between her café and the abandoned field. His fingers slipped away. The red chrome popcorn machine he'd dug out from the back of his shop was waiting in the yard under a canopy, but that wasn't all he'd done.

"I know it's not perfect, but I really did try my best."

"Oh, Dad!" Julia didn't know where to look. "It *is* perfect."

A wooden frame of red and yellow arched around the entrance to the small yard, but it was the smoky flashing bulbs of the large 'POPCORN' sign propped on the wall that drew the eyes of the festivalgoers already in need of the blue port-a-loos, conveniently positioned behind the post office next door.

"People are going to be walking past here *all* day," he said, just as giddy as Katie had been to show off her salon. "Vinnie helped paint the wood. All scrap from the abandoned builder's yard behind my shop. The sign was a little harder to track down, but a friend of a friend's brother's uncle is a juggler in a travelling circus, and it's ours for the weekend. And that's not all!"

He ushered Julia into the small yard and patted a stack of blue coolers. "They're filled with water bottles, on account of all the salt and sugar. And if you'll follow me." He pushed the back door to the kitchen, where a mountain of bagged kernels awaited on the island. "Same stuff they use at the cinema. Called in a favour, so it's basically pure profit." He pulled a bag from the pile and tossed it to Julia, nodding to the orderly line already forming under the flashing sign. "It seems your crowd awaits."

The first act to take the stage was a poet giving a dramatic reading over strange techno beats that Julia was sure would thin the crowd. But as singers replaced the poets, it only continued to grow, until the back of the dancing crowd met the impatient lines at the port-a-loos.

Packet after packet of the kernels went into the kettle only to emerge as fluffy pieces of popcorn. No matter how quickly she refilled, Julia couldn't keep the popcorn in the machine as bag after bag went out with sprinkles of salt, sugar, and often both. Her father managed to upsell water to at least every third person while he took their money.

The work was constant, but as she spent it standing in one place, it might have been the most leisurely afternoon she'd ever had the pleasure of working. The thumping music, along with as many handfuls of popcorn as she could sneak, were helping keep her energy levels up. She'd tried to resist for the sake of sales, but nothing beat the hot, fresh stuff.

"Well, I was certainly wrong about this," Dot said when she turned up not long after noon, her neck stretching to look at the length of the queue trailing along the footpath. "Go and take a break. Percy and I will take over for an hour."

Julia and her father leaned against the outside wall and looked out to the field while a DJ duo wearing clown masks remixed songs that she recognised from her early days of watching kid's TV. Julia couldn't resist joining the crowd as they roared the lyrics to a club-ready version of the *Chucklevision* theme tune. She looked to her father as it bled into *The Magic Roundabout*, but he was too busy flicking through their takings.

"And there's still hours to go," he said, tucking it away with a smile as wide as the Cheshire Cat. "This day couldn't be going any better. You're going to be swimming in..."

His attention drifted to his ringing mobile phone.

"It's Clive."

"Who?"

"Clive Winston," he said. "That old record producer friend I told you about. You met him once."

He tapped the green button with a grin. "*Clive!* How are things? You're in the village?"

"That I am." Julia could hear him. "Look, Brian, are you at that manor you shacked up in? We're having some lodging issues."

Julia followed the sound of Clive's voice to the alley when she realised that she wasn't hearing his booming voice through the phone. Pacing among the people still filtering towards the field, he was rubbing between his brows. With blown-back hair and an open shirt showing off a hairy chest, Julia might have mistaken him for her father at a glance.

"*Clive!*" Brian called, hanging up as he joined Julia. "Good to see you, old friend! How many years has it been?"

"Erm..." Clive scratched his neck before he took Brian's hands. "Too long, pal. Too long. Listen, as I was just saying, I don't suppose you have rooms going spare at your manor?"

"I'm afraid not. Had to sell the place."

"Fallen on hard times?" He laughed, slapping Brian's arm. "Spare room?"

"It's not the biggest of cottages."

"Hmm." Rubbing his stubble, Clive searched the alley. "All the B&Bs and hotels are booked for miles, and I've got one demanding band with nowhere to stay. What about you?" He directed this to Julia. "Got a spare room?"

"You remember, Julia, don't you?" Brian said. "She must have only been about my Vinnie's age when you met."

Clive squinted at her, and she could tell he didn't remember her. She didn't take it personally. As far as she was concerned, she'd never seen the man before. Behind him, Shilpa and Evelyn were offering themselves for pat-downs behind the turnstile.

"Right, yeah." Still squinting, he shook her hand limply. "Spitting image. I thought she was that young lass you married for a second, you lucky swine." He laughed again, though Brian only offered a light chuckle. "Spare room?"

"Jett!" Shilpa cried.

Julia and her father looked upwards, but Shilpa's eyes were trained on the bottom of the alley as she hurried down in a bright pink sari. Evelyn was still being patted down as she took off her jumble of crystal necklaces. Julia followed Shilpa's stunned gaze to a black bus with darkened windows parked between the toilets and the post office.

A man with an open leather jacket who'd forgotten to put on a shirt ran his fingers through oily blonde hair darkened at the roots. The word "MUSIC" was tattooed under his navel in a sagging arch. A couple of passers-by pointed their phones in his direction, but most ignored him as they streamed forward.

"Julia, don't you know who that is?" Shilpa could barely get the words out. "That's *the* Jett Fury. Lead singer of Electric Fury!"

"I think I heard them on the radio," she said, remembering the blush pink buttercream. "You're a fan?"

"A *fan*?" Shilpa couldn't take her eyes away. "I saw their first show. What must it have been? Twenty years ago?"

"A woman of taste, I see." Clive offered his hand to Shilpa with a sickly-sweet smile. "Clive Winston. Producer, agent, manager, and whatever else His Highness wants of me – and right now, he wants somewhere to stay. Don't suppose you've got a spare room going?"

"I don't."

"Dammit."

"But I do have a small flat empty."

"You do?" Clive's eyes lit up. "Not far, is it?"

"Right behind you." Shilpa pointed at the red door that led above the post office. "That's only if Julia doesn't mind? Still a few months till Jessie gets back."

"Who's Julia?" Clive asked.

"Right here," she said. "We just met."

"Ah, yes. Well, do you mind?"

"I mean, I suppose—"

"Excellent!" Clive wrapped his arm around Shilpa's shoulder and set off towards the bus. "I think we can come to some sort of arrangement..."

At the van, Shilpa fawned over *the* Jett Fury, who barely raised a smile to her squealing. Clive slapped on the bus, and a woman in a metallic dress and a fur coat stumbled off, eyes hidden behind giant saucer shades. A much younger woman with distinct black piercings settled into dimples on either side of her cheeks follower her. Neither woman looked old enough to have been in a band twenty years ago. Julia assumed the younger of the two was their roadie, given the number of bags she had crammed under each arm.

"I've sorted us a small flat." Clive waved them towards the red door. "Shilpy here has kindly offered it."

"Shilpa," she corrected as she unlocked the door. "Just stay out of the drawers."

"What a dump." Jett dragged gold aviators into his oily hair to show deep crow's feet wrapping around bloodshot eyes. Julia would have guessed he was closer to fifty than forty. "You promised us a manor, Clive."

"When isn't Clive talking hot air?" said the woman

with the fur as she glanced over her glasses, not bothering to hide the wrinkle in her nose as she looked around the alley. "As long as it has a bathtub, I don't care at this point. I can't spend another second on that bus."

"No bath, I'm afraid," Shilpa called as she followed them up the stairs. "There is a shower, but the water pressure isn't the…"

The youngest of the trio struggled down the alley with the bags. Julia rushed to help her, but she tugged away and trudged up the stairs, kicking the door shut behind her.

"They seem…" Julia searched for the right word. "Nice?"

"*Brian!*" Dot's voice called them back to the yard. "This piece of junk is on the fritz!"

Julia ran under the flashing bulbs as they faded in and out to find the light behind the smoked glass of the popcorn machine doing the same. Dot gave it a hefty wallop, but it wasn't only the popcorn machine. The music cut out, followed by the crowd's immediate booing. Julia looked around the festival as the fading lights flickered.

The disruption only lasted a few seconds before the lights and sound returned to normal. The folk band who'd replaced the DJ duo, and wouldn't have sounded out of place playing on a farm, apologised for the technical difficulties, and the booing became roaring cheers once more.

"Just a blip," Brian said, taking over from Percy at the water station. "Should we carry on, Julia? Popcorn to sell."

5

*T*he electricity faded in and out twice more over the course of the day, and after a passing shower dumped a cloud full of rain over the festival, the ease of the afternoon drifted away with it.

"I'll have two shots of sambuca," a young man with a tongue piercing shouted over the music in Julia's ear, soaked from the rain, "pink, if you've got it ... and ... and ... you got the time?"

"About six," Brian called.

"About six," she parroted.

Clutching Julia's shoulder for balance, he waved at a girl too interested in recording herself with a flower crown blossoming throughout her blue hair on the screen. The crown was a filter, but the blue hair was real as blue hair got.

"You want some prosecco, Georgia?"

"We're selling popcorn."

"*Popcorn*?" He recoiled, staring at the pink bags with eyes that couldn't entirely focus. "I suppose I should eat."

"I insist you do."

And on it went.

The closer to sunset they crept, the drunker the festivalgoers seemed to get. Once the police started carting people away in handcuffs, it didn't take long for the madness to spread to the popcorn line.

"You stepped on my foot!"

"Maybe *your* foot shouldn't have been under *my* foot."

After the first sloppy fist was thrown, Julia jumped at her father's suggestion to end their day. They shut the gate, pulled down the sign, and dragged the machine into the kitchen, where less than half their stock of kernels remained. Once everything was locked up, she could only think about crawling into a bubble bath and tucking into the pizza Barker had promised they'd order on her return.

"Not bad for a day's work, eh?" Brian snapped an elastic band around a thick wedge of rolled notes. "Fifty percent, my behind. The cheek of them."

They walked down the alley, and Julia was

surprised to see Shilpa chomping on her nails while leaning next to the flat door.

"Evelyn wandered off hours ago with a tambourine, and I haven't seen her since," she said, checking her watch. "Give that door another knock, will you? He's going to be late."

Julia knocked on the flat door.

"Late for what?"

"Clive's letting me watch their rehearsal at the village hall. Can you believe it?" Her foot tapped. "Starts in five minutes, and I promised I'd make sure Jett was there for eight. I've been trying for ten minutes. I think he might have fallen asleep."

Footsteps bombed down the stairway behind the door. It ripped open, and a girl in a black hood stumbled out. As the girl barged into Julia's father, more footsteps rushed down the stairs. She fell to the ground, as did the money roll from Brian's hand. She snatched it up and turned towards the field as Jett blasted through the door, with a towel clutched below his tattoo, dripping head to toe.

"I don't think so!" He blocked her path. "You're not getting away with it this time."

Jett hopped from side to side, but she was nimble. Cash clenched in her fist, she met Julia's eyes with a smirk as a strand of creamy blue hair fell from under the hood.

They recognised each other.

Julia had given her directions on her journey past the cottage almost a week ago. The same girl whose friend had tried to buy a bottle of prosecco while she'd been busy recording herself. Julia grabbed for the girl, but she was too quick. She darted around them, evading Shilpa and Brian's snatching hands. The security guards at the turnstiles were busy looking in the opposite direction as the young girl scaled the metal walls.

"She's called Georgia," Julia said as they hurried to the alley's opening.

"And I've got a restraining order against that psycho," Jett cried. "She's been stalking me all year."

Jett looked around, noticing the half a dozen people recording him. He shoved past a woman holding her phone and back into the flat.

"Don't forget the rehearsal at the village hall!" Shilpa called after him.

"Please tell me that wasn't all the money, Dad?"

"It wasn't all the money," he said, as Georgia sprinted around the metal maze while the security guards followed at a crawl. "But it was all of the cash. Still have the card payments. I'm sorry, love. She came at me like a bat out of hell."

Jett stomped down the stairs, back in his leather jacket, his jeans swapped for leather pants.

He'd still forgotten his shirt and, this time, his shoes.

"Must be difficult having a stalker," she said.

"Comes with the territory."

"*This way!*" Shilpa scooped her arm around Jett's and pulled him towards the turnstiles. "Mr Fury, like I said before, I'm such a huge fan of your music. Can I ask about what inspired your latest..."

"Oi, you!" Brian cried, waving to one of the many patrolling officers. "Didn't you see what just happened? I'd like to report a theft!"

Rather than following her father, Julia hurried to catch up with Jett and Shilpa. How long before the pink glow of her friend's fanaticism wore off? Given what Julia had seen from the rockstar so far, it was only a matter of time before he fell off his pedestal.

Waved over by Clive smoking a cigar in the vestibule of St. Peter's Church, Shilpa and Jett headed there instead of the village hall. Jett hurried straight in, and Shilpa followed behind like a puppy.

"Jett insisted on having the best acoustics," he explained to Julia. "We've met..."

"Julia. Brian's daughter?"

"Right. Of course." He shook her hand in both of

his. Dragging them away, his fingers were as coarse and dry as sandpaper. Had the man never heard of hand cream? "Long day, do forgive me. I've been here, there, and would you believe it, everywhere."

"You can't smoke in here. There's a sign right behind you."

"Ceilings go up forever." He wafted the cigar around between two thick fingers. "These are some grand old buildings, eh, Brian?"

Julia turned to see her father catching up.

"Police are bloody useless around here," he muttered. "They might as well have told me there was nothing they could do. You can't smoke in here, Clive."

"Bet there's more than a few bobs worth of tat knocking around in the vestry, eh, old pal? Still in antiques? I'll give you my ex-wife's number."

A laugh boomed over the sound of an electric guitar, his hand slapping Brian's arm.

"C'mon, Clive." Brian nodded at the sign. "Have a bit of respect."

"Alright, alright!" Clive lifted his dry hands, puffing all the way to the door. "Keep your hair on, fella. I get it. You village folk are something, I'll give you that. Can't blame a man for celebrating."

Half-leaning into the church, the smoke came through with his words all the same.

"Don't suppose you've seen any people that look

like record label scouts knocking around the place?" He puffed like a chimney as his smile stretched. "If this lot doesn't go off-script, we're heading for the big leagues after tonight. We're in the money…"

Clive wandered off, humming a cheerful tune to himself.

Inside the lofty church, the old wood and spices were too thick in the air to be affected by the cigar. The rehearsal space had been set up at the end of the aisle where Julia, and half the village, had said their wedding vows over the years.

Jett was perched on a speaker near the left pews, where Shilpa was hanging on his every movement as his fingers plucked and tuned at a gold electric guitar. From the empty thuds, he'd yet to plug in. Two microphone stands had been set up on a network of worn-out overlaid rugs, with a drum kit to the right side. The girl with the dimple piercings was lost in her phone behind the drums, sticks already in hand.

Not the roadie, after all.

"Whatever he's telling you," called the woman with the fur coat, leaning against the wooden lectern with a white guitar around her neck, "don't believe it. I fell for it all once too."

"Hilarious, Mix," he said without looking up. "Would you excuse my wife? She has a rotten sense of humour."

"You must be massaging his ego," the woman named Mix shrugged off her fur coat. She was in her metal dress from earlier, and from the jangling, it appeared to be made entirely of safety pins. "It's the only time you'll ever see him truly smile."

"Shut it, Mix."

"No."

Brian let out a strained chuckle, but nobody else was laughing. Their words were banter-like in nature, but Julia couldn't imagine talking with Barker in the same acid-laced tones.

"*Sticks*!" Jett called loudly as he walked over to the drums, waving his hands over his head. "I don't pay you to sit on your phone."

"Bite me." Her voice was careful and slow, her hands signing a complicated string of words. "And you *know* my name is Tia."

"I prefer Sticks."

"Mumbler." Tia jerked her thumb at Julia. "Who's this lot?"

"I was just thinking the same thing," said Mix. "Closed rehearsal."

"Think Clive has sent them in to spy on me." Jett adjusted the central microphone stand. "But what my *darling* wife said, closed rehearsal."

"We were just leaving." Julia was glad to. "Good luck with the show."

"There's no luck involved." A smile twisted Jett's cheeks into lines. "It's all talent and—" His feet squelched, still as barefoot as when he'd left the flat. "These rugs are soaked!"

"Churches are cold," Mix said.

"But it's *not* cold." He wriggled his toes. "It's literally soaking."

"Mine's fine," Mix said, tuning her guitar like Jett, with quicker fingers. "We don't have time for this. Let's just run 'Lightning in a Bottle' from the top." Her eyes went to Shilpa. "What did I say about a *closed* rehearsal?"

Tia twirled the sticks artfully and she gave the drums a once over. The drumming seemed skilful, but the overlapping echoes bouncing around the church didn't sound pleasant to Julia's ears.

"I saw Jax," said Mix as they were walking away.

"Why would you say that *right* now?" she heard Jett shout. "Are you trying to get in my head?"

"Oh, because the *whole* world revolves around you?"

Tia's drumming intensified.

"You're lying."

"Okay, I'm lying." Mix laughed. "But I *did* see him. Let's just keep living under delusions why don't—"

With Tia soundtracking their argument, Julia didn't hear the rest as they walked back up the aisle.

"Well, the stars certainly do act different," Shilpa said once they were outside. "Oh, there she is! Over here, Evelyn!"

Shilpa rushed off, leaving Julia to wonder how Shilpa could be unaffected by Jett's display. She supposed it was a good thing someone was enjoying themselves. Letting out a yawn, Julia was ready to crawl into bed, having seen enough of Electric Fury to know she was fine missing their headlining performance.

"Have they started yet?" Clive marched at them, weaving around a couple deep in an argument and another throwing up next to the metal wall. "They're meant to be on in twenty."

"Oh, they started," she said. "From the second they saw each other."

"Lover's tiff. Nothing to worry your pretty little head about."

Though Julia was smiling, her jaw was clenched.

Clive Winston had been getting on her nerves since she'd met him.

"Watch how you talk to my daughter, Clive." Brian's firmness as he folded his arms surprised Julia; this time, he didn't humour his old friend with a shred of politeness. "She's got more brains between her ears than the two of us combined."

"No harm meant by it. Just old fashioned in my ways, is all."

Clive tipped his cigar to them, glancing at Julia without meeting her eyes before walking back through the gates. She could only imagine what he was muttering under his breath as he went into the church.

"I should go and see how Katie's first day at the salon went." He pulled her into a tight hug. "I'll keep hounding the police until that money turns up."

"I think they're right about it being as good as gone."

"I am sorry, love. I should have kept a tighter grip on it."

"Not your fault."

"Same time tomorrow?"

"Only if you're sure?"

"This lot aren't going to be buying antiques, are they? I meant what I said. I'll never be done saying thank you for how much you've guided Katie. Nobody else—"

A bang as loud as a cannon startled them both, turning them back to St. Peter's as the lights cut out behind the stained glass. The church's pylon wires fizzed towards the bushes on the other side of the village hall. The greenery hummed a flat, low note, and something inside exploded. The green metal door of the electrical station burst through the shrubs. It bounced over the church wall in a twisting somersault, narrowly missing the young couple who'd been arguing seconds earlier.

People scrambled back from the flaming bushes, and Brian yanked Julia against the metal cage. Not for the first time that day, the music stopped, and the booing of thousands quickly followed.

Clive stumbled from the church with a pallid complexion. Ash trailed from his mouth as the cigar toppled from his lips and down the steps. Judging by his staggering gait, Julia wondered if he'd been shot, but there was no sign of an entry wound or even a drop of blood.

Behind him, smoke drifted out, and it wasn't from the cigar. The scent reminded Julia of the barbeque smell that had filled Peridale over the summer, only so thick that it smelled like two dozen families had roasted their afternoon away.

And there was something else.

A metallic hint.

Clive fell to his knees on the top step, and Julia ran towards the echoing screaming from within the church that hadn't eased off in pitch or consistency. As the smoke cleared, Mix and Tia were where she'd left them. Mix was the one screaming, guitar dangling from her neck as she half-bent forward, hands clasped at her mouth.

Behind the drums, Tia was silently staring.

The microphone in the centre of the rugs melted in two, sagging down to a smouldering mass that Julia could only assume was *the* Jett Fury.

6

*"E*LECTROCUTED FURY!'" Dot slapped the folded newspaper down on Julia's breakfast bar the following morning in the dim kitchen. "'The power of music kills festival headliner, Jett Fury, during an ELECTRIFYING rehearsal!' Johnny must get a kick out of writing these."

"After what happened last night, the headline wrote itself." Barker let out an awkward laugh as he poured boiled water from a saucepan into a French press. "It's made the rounds in the national press too. Most I could find written about them outside a few local paper reviews for their shows. They were a strange band."

"Very odd name."

"I'm not talking about the name. They were big

59

enough to get a headline spot, but I couldn't find any recorded music from them. No streaming, CDs, or vinyl, only live performances."

"Well, *I'd* never heard of them," Dot said with a wave of her hand. "Then again, I'd never heard of any of the people on the line-up."

"And yet everyone else had *something* I could buy."

"They're never going to get the chance now," said Dot. "The Beatles didn't carry on without John, did they?"

"They had been split up by a decade by then."

"Such a tragic way to go."

Julia hadn't been able to rid the smoky sight from her mind's eye. She reached the back of the refrigerator's top shelf for the soft cheese. It went into the bin bag with the rest of the fridge's contents.

"I think the council should reimburse everybody in Peridale for all this food waste," Dot said on Julia's return from the outside bin. "Mind you, in my day, we wouldn't have thrown everything away at the drop of a hat. We weren't so picky."

Julia chose tact as Barker slurped his coffee with the amused look he often were around his grandmother-in-law. "I don't think it's the council's fault that my food spoiled."

"Isn't it?" Dot fanned the paper. Olivia found this amusing, laughing porridge onto her chin. "The whole village is without power right now. Johnny made some *excellent* points in his article. There's a reason we've never had a festival in Peridale before. Of all the reasons I thought this was a bad idea, I never thought it would be our poor electrics that couldn't handle it. I don't want to say I told you so—"

"Then don't," said Barker.

"But I *knew* I should have put my foot down and protested. That poor man *exploded* right before your eyes, Julia."

"He didn't explode, and even if he had, I didn't *see* it happen." Julia heard an echo of buzzing as she hovered over the peppermint and liquorice teabags in the cupboard. Coffee it was. "Cup of tea, Gran?"

"I thought you'd never offer." Dot cut eyes at the cat clock. It was only half past seven. "And I never thought you of all people would be on the council's side. I hope they're not waiting until Monday to take down what's left of that monstrosity on the green."

"What's left?" Julia asked.

"Didn't you hear them last night?" she cried. "The police telling thousands of people on the drink and *who knows* what that they were shutting down the festival was never going to end well. They started ripping those metal fences down with their bare hands. Pure savagery, if ever I've seen it."

"Is my café—"

"Don't worry, dear," she said quickly. "We were on watch all night. My megaphone kept them away. Couldn't stop the post office from getting a bin through the window, though, and Richie's Bar might as well start again with the renovations. Oh, it was such a frightful display. Of course, we'll do our best as a neighbourhood watch to put things right, but part of me is wondering if we should just leave it so the council can see what they've done. Bunch of self-interested swine. The lot of them need to go *now*!"

"Did you vote in the by-election?" asked Barker

Dot's attention went to wiping Olivia's porridge-coated chin. "Well, erm, I was busy that day. But what I said stands. They don't care about us, and it's becoming clearer by the day. Don't forget that they tried to sell off our library. And here we are still sitting in the dark drinking tea from boiled water like we never left the caves."

"I thought things were better in your day?" said Barker. "Although you're right about this being their mess *if* this was an accident."

"If?" Dot directed this at Julia, who hid the almond milk as she added a splash into her gran's tea. "You know I'm not one to gossip, but—"

"Do I?"

"But I don't think anything fishy happened," Dot

continued. "And neither do most people. The electrics have been dodgy for *years*, and yesterday only proved it. You saw it fading in and out with your own two eyes."

Julia couldn't recall the last sustained power cut aside from the blips the day before. "I'm sure you're right. Something that tragic surely can't have been planned."

She wriggled her toes against the cold kitchen tiles, still damp from where she'd spilt some water while carrying the pan to the stove. Stirring the tea, she hoped for once that the rumours weren't too far wrong, for once.

"Mark my words, Julia." She was glad her gran always needed to fill the silence. "We'll find out Jett Fury's death was nothing more than an unfortunate accident, and this power cut will drag out for days." She sipped her tea. "Oh, gosh, that is foul. What in heavens did you—"

A knock sent Julia into the hallway, but her gran overtook and yanked open the door. Detective Inspector John Christie turned around, puffing on his electronic cigarette. Barker's former colleague looked like he hadn't slept.

"Well?" Dot demanded with folded arms. "Was it an accident?"

"We're looking into several possibilities, and good

morning to you too, Dorothy." John ducked into the cottage, looking straight at Julia. "A word?"

DI Christie nodded to Barker on his way to the dining room, though he shut the door behind Julia before he could join them. He offered Julia a seat, but she decided to stay standing.

"I gave my statement last night."

"Relax, Julia," he said, loosening his crinkled tie. "I'm just here to check over some things. I've had the night from hell. This band is a tricky bunch. They're all sticking to the same story."

"And that story is?"

"I'm not here to feed into your obsession with local crime," he said, collapsing into the seat Julia hadn't taken. He pulled out his notepad and flicked a few pages. "You said you saw Jett's toes wriggling in water on the rug?"

"I did."

"You're the only one."

"Are you sure?" Julia dragged out the chair across from him and sat down. "That can't be right. Ask Shilpa, ask my father."

"I did. Shilpa had a lot to say about his lovely blue eyes, but she didn't notice if he was wearing shoes or not, and your father said a stone pillar was blocking his view."

"And Mix and Tia?"

"I can barely get a word from the wife." He rubbed at his brow. "I'm giving her the benefit of the doubt that she's in shock, but she says she didn't look. She's also claiming that she loved her husband dearly, and Shilpa and your father didn't take the way they were acting with each other the same way as you. The manager was outside at that moment on a phone call, which we've already confirmed through the logs. The drummer is deaf and claims not to have known anything about the rug being wet because they had their backs to her. She didn't have any comments about their relationship. She hasn't been in the band long."

"But he *was* barefoot on a wet rug." Frowning at the table, Julia listened to her swirling thoughts. "Which can only mean it was murder, considering how he died."

"You know what church roofs are like, and we had that shower earlier in the day. By your own report, you saw him in a towel. He could have dripped that water himself."

"The rug was soaked. He was slightly damp. What about the church's electrics?"

"As old and dodgy as the roof," he said, tucking his notepad away. "Forensics are going over the place as we speak. That's all I wanted to check regarding your statement."

"Unless you have an update about the stolen money, this could have been a phone call."

"The video footage we picked up confirmed it was Jett's stalker. Georgia Kingsley, seventeen, from Portsmouth. For someone so young, she's certainly a handful. Checked into the B&B on Sunday, the day after Electric Fury announced they'd still be headlining even with the location change. But just being in the same village as Jett broke the restraining order the courts granted him. She's been making his life hell, from the sounds of it."

"Doing what?"

"You're right, this could have been a phone call. That's not the only reason I'm here." Sighing, he pushed himself out of the chair as Julia did the same. "Two more things, both unofficial. First, I'm going to need you to keep your nose out."

"A little presumptuous, don't you think?"

"Considering who you are, no." Christie's lips vanished into a tight line before taking a sideways blast of his e-cigarette. "Given the names involved, I have eyes on me right now who could have my guts for garters if I make one little misstep. I don't need you or your nosy family," he said louder, and there was a grumble at the door, "messing this up for me. Given how many statements we had about the issues with the

66

electricity all over the village yesterday, an accidental death would be the best result for everyone."

For everyone but Jett, if it wasn't an accident, she thought.

"You're doing it."

"Doing what?"

"Already thinking way too much about it." He circled her face with his e-cig. "*That* look always leads to trouble. Just stay out of this, okay?"

"The second thing, Detective Inspector?"

He pulled out the chair again.

"You might want to sit down for this one."

"Just spit it out, John."

"Things got a little out of hand after the shutdown," he said, tugging his tie further. "We tried our best to contain things, but we were outnumbered hundreds to one, even with every officer in the county turning up in riot gear. I'm sorry to be the bearer of bad news, but I hope you have insurance for your café."

Julia's throat closed, and she said, "I do."

"And *why* does she need it?" Dot burst in, clearly having been listening at the door the whole time. "I saw the café myself, and it was in excellent shape when I left my cottage not thirty minutes ago."

"From the front, yes." Another sigh and his eyes

67

went to the carpet. "You might want to go and have a look. Really, I am sorry."

With the strewn metal fences and ripped-up red mats, the village green looked like a tornado had ripped through. Wooden boards blocked the windows of the post office and Richie's Bar, which was missing half of its scaffolding.

Julia's Café looked untouched behind one of the few undisrupted metal fence panels. She sprinted around the workers in polo shirts branded with the festival logo. She thrust through the turnstile and down the alley, ignoring their calls to stop.

The gate had been kicked in, and the kitchen window smashed. The back door hung on one hinge, and kernels had been strewn everywhere in the kitchen. The popcorn machine and sign were nowhere in sight, and every plate and bowl were nothing more than scattered shards of porcelain. From the spread, they'd had fun throwing them around.

But it was the café where the most damage had been done. She flicked on the light switch, forgetting the power was still out. Walking over the destruction, she yanked up the blind she'd rolled down on

Wednesday night when her biggest problem had been having to close for a few days.

"Oh my goodness." Dot's voice was barely above a whisper as light flooded in, and she had Olivia's face against her shoulder. "Julia, if I'd known they were coming in through the back…"

"There'd have been nothing you could have done to stop it."

The glass cabinets had been smashed to smithereens, and the tables and chairs broken down to nothing more than firewood, but the walls were the hardest to look at. The pink and blue cupcake print wallpaper might as well have not been there behind the overlapping swathes of multi-coloured spray paint. There were no designs or personal tags, just pointless, aimless scribbles bleeding from the walls to the ceiling and floor.

To add insult to injury, the power finally returned to show the mess in its full glory.

"Well," she said, gulping past a hard, dry lump, "I have to say, it's never looked better."

Beneath the café in Barker's windowless private investigator office, Julia accepted a cup of peppermint and liquorice tea with unsteady hands.

She sipped her old favourite, usually such a comfort, but it did nothing to rid her of the anguish chewing her up. Someone was sweeping glass above, raising her out of the creaky leather chesterfield sofa. Barker forced her back down, wrapping his hand around hers.

"I should be helping."

"Just take a moment," he said softly. "I don't care how long it takes. I will track down everyone who did this and make them pay for what they've done."

"You're a good PI, Barker, but you'd have an easier time trying to separate salt and sugar." She sipped the tea, and at least the hot water was a distraction. "It wouldn't make a difference. The damage has been done."

"We won't stop until it's exactly as it was."

"I should have just taken a few weeks off to figure out a plan, like you said."

"And this would probably still have happened," he said, pulling her close. "There was no rhyme or reason. No cause to fight for; just angry people doing what angry people do when things don't go their way. I just spoke to Shilpa. The post office was looted clean, and there are smashed windows up and down Mulberry Lane."

"Is Katie's—"

"Untouched," he cut in. "According to your gran,

your father was scaring people off with a cricket bat all night. You can't blame yourself."

Clenching her eyes, Julia knew he was right. Blaming herself didn't make the feeling go away, and more tears forced their way out as she heard her gran shouting orders above.

"You're right," she said, balancing the tea on the chair arm. "And it seems I've got those few weeks anyway. The café isn't going to come together overnight. I assume you were listening to what John was saying?"

"Glass against the wall in the bedroom," he admitted. "Your gran was hogging the door. I could tell you didn't think it was an accident before he turned up, and neither do I, failing electrics or not. John will do what John always does. He'll try to save his backside, and if everything points to an accidental death, so will he."

"Everything?" Julia couldn't help but shake her head. "Not even close. You didn't see how they were all acting. I saw four people who didn't seem to like each other very much. When you throw in a stalker with a restraining order who's been in the village for almost a week, I think this was anything but accidental."

"Are you saying what I think you're saying?"

"If this was a freak accident, why is Jett the only one dead?" She looked off into the darkness of the basement as her mind drifted back to the rehearsal at the church. "Everyone who could have been behind this came to the village because of Jett. We just have to figure out which one wanted him dead."

"Considering she's done a runner, I say we start by finding out what Georgia did to get a restraining order against her."

"Good place to start," she said, though she'd gone to someone else first. "There are people who were closer to Jett who'll be able to help build up a picture of why someone would want to hurt him."

Glancing up at the ceiling, he whispered, "For the sake of our sanity, let's keep this one between us."

7

*H*olding a stack of cling-film wrapped glass baking dishes the following morning, Julia looked to St. Peter's Church from the alley's opening. Forensics were still crawling all over the place as the festival organisers continued their breakdown of the structures. DI Christie glanced in her direction as he shooed four people dressed all in black from laying flowers outside the church.

At least the police were still exploring their options.

Leaving them to it, she approached the flat. Like the previous Sunday, she'd spent the morning in her kitchen, though she hadn't needed to reach for the sugar or food colouring this week. She knocked, and the door swung inwards, the yale lock on the latch.

Scratchy guitar plucks poured from the black tour bus, still parked behind the post office, but she chose to proceed to the flat.

"Hello?" Julia called as she reached the top of the stairs.

Mix was at the small dining table between the open plan kitchen and living area. She slapped a leather binder shut as Julia took in the flat. It was a mess, even by Jessie's standards, but her daughter had never covered half of the clothes-strewn cream sofa in a large red stain.

"It's wine," Mix said quickly, rising from the creaky chair. "What are you doing in here?"

"I'm Julia. We briefly met the other day. I was in the red dress?"

"I remember. My question still stands. What do you want?"

"I made you some meals," she said, sliding the stack onto the table. She glanced at the leather binder's gold 'CONTRACTS' label. "Cottage pie, lasagne, and a chicken vegetable tray bake. Cooking instructions are on the post-its."

"You still haven't answered my question."

Folding her arms, Mix's brows darted up. Julia hadn't expected a warm reception, but she'd hoped the home cooking would smooth out their introductions.

"This is my daughter's flat," she said as Mix started clearing away the clothes that had made their way around. "I wanted to make sure you were all eating properly, considering what happened. I really am sorry for your loss. It might be a silly question, but how are you holding up?"

"You're right. It is a silly question." Mix shot daggers at her. "And don't think I don't know that you're one of *them*."

Them?

Julia's mind went straight to Peridale's Ears.

Had her gran already taken a stab at interviewing Jett's widow?

"One of Jett's side pieces," Mix continued with a strained laugh. "*Convenient* that we'd end up in your daughter's flat, don't you think? Get out."

"Oh, no, Mix, you've got the wrong—"

"*Get out!*"

"I'm married." Julia held up her left hand. "Two years this Christmas. Look at the wall behind you. That's us with our daughter, Jessie, on our wedding day. I swear, I only met Jett on Friday, and I barely said two words to him. I just wanted to see how you were doing, but I can see this is a bad time. I'll go."

Julia hoped the food would be enough to get her back through the door on a calmer day.

"Wait!" Mix called, her scratchy voice softening.

"It's been a strange couple of days. I don't know how to handle any of this. I'm sorry."

"No need to apologise." Julia rolled up her sleeves and looked around the flat. "Clear somewhere for us to sit, and I'll put the kettle on."

The open-plan kitchen at the back of the flat was just as much of a mess. However, judging by the stack of pizza boxes and yellow takeaway cartons, it didn't look like anyone had attempted to cook.

It was almost like Jessie was home.

While the kettle boiled, Julia ripped a bin bag off a roll and cleared away as much as possible. She'd spent much of the previous day doing the same next door. Julia joined Mix in the sitting room with two cups of tea and half a packet of slightly stale custard creams left behind in the cupboard. Mix had cleared the sofa of clothes, but she was standing at the wedding picture, chewing on her black-painted fingernails.

"Same church," she remarked. "Looks low key, even for a village wedding."

"That was our second attempt. The first was..." Julia paused, wondering if she should mention that the choirmaster had dropped dead during the ceremony mere feet from where Jett had done the same. "...derailed. Just close friends and family the second time."

"Was it nice?"

76

Smiling, she nodded, but Mix's eyes went down to her left hand.

There was no ring and no indent left behind by one.

"He wasn't a romantic," she said, taking the tea from Julia. "I used to like that about him. The men Mother and Father set me up with always tried rather too hard to impress me. Yachts, diamonds, bigger yachts, bigger diamonds, even bigger yachts." Tucking her feet under herself in the corner of the sofa, she stared blankly into the tea. "We got married at the registry office on a tour date in Great Yarmouth. Paid a random man we found drunk on the pier a tenner to be our witness, but that's rock'n'roll, baby."

"I can't imagine life on the road is easy?"

"Far from it, but it was the only life he would live. When we met, he told me as much, and I was ready to run away. Or was I kicked out? I can't remember." Gaze distant, she took another sip before snapping back. "Mother and Father were right about me. A waste of good breeding. 'You'll never amount to anything, Vivi.'"

"There's still plenty of time to prove them wrong," Julia said, offering a smile that was barely returned. "Is Mix a nickname?"

"It's what he called me," she said, lip snarling. "Always in the mix, always keeping things ticking along. You name it, I did it. Said the band couldn't keep going without me, and I used to believe him. I always knew people only came to see us because of him, but now I suppose we'll find out if that's the case."

"Electric Fury is continuing?"

Quick thuds came up the stairs, and Tia, the drummer with the cheek piercings, hurried in with two steaming pizza boxes. She hesitated, her dark eyes even more distrusting than Mix's had been. She placed one pizza box on the back of the sofa before retreating into the kitchen. Her trained stare didn't leave Julia.

"I said *no* pineapple," Mix muttered to herself, slapping the box shut before tossing it onto the coffee table. "And we're going to try. None of us has much choice. Not qualified to do much of anything else. The songs are still *the* songs, and the fans love them. He was a good songwriter. I'll give him that. Could create an earworm like nobody's business. People might come out just to listen to them. But like I said, he *was* the band as far as he was concerned. We stood in the back, and if he wasn't in one of his moods with me, he'd turn my microphone on so I could do backing vocals."

"Was he often in moods?"

"That's rock'n'roll, baby," she repeated, and Julia

could almost hear Jett's voice echoing through. "He went from a rough childhood to rough adolescence to a terrible record deal, to finally taking the reins and starting his own thing away from everything and everyone. I wasn't the only one running."

"How did you meet?"

"Somehow, Electric Fury was booked to play at one of Father's hunter's balls," she said, smiling at the memory. "I think it was someone's idea of a windup. A bit of rough to entertain Father's friends. I don't think he expected me to fall in love. Jett promised me the world that night, and I didn't hesitate to jump on his bus with him."

The smile soured into a snarl, her gaze drifting away again.

"The rehearsal," Julia pushed. "I heard it was supposed to be at the village hall?"

"Jett wanted to change. That's what I heard."

"And demands like that weren't out of the ordinary?"

"Since I've been in the band, there hasn't been a single show where there hasn't been some drama about one thing or another."

"But never one that resulted in death."

"Obviously not." Mix's eyes narrowed on Julia. "An accident, according to the police."

"Yes, I've been hearing that too," she said,

wondering how best to approach the niggling question that had kept her awake late into the night. "Moving all that equipment must have been a pain, surely? Something could have been set up wrong?"

"Mix?" Tia called from the kitchen. "A word?"

Mix sprung off the sofa without hesitation and went to Tia. After some quietly exchanged words, Mix glared back, any shred of friendliness gone.

Julia knew she'd pushed too far.

"Get out!" Mix demanded again, harsher than the first. "You forgot to mention that your husband is a PI. Tia saw you coming out of his office last night. Who sent you?"

"Nobody, we're just interested in—"

"You know what, quite frankly, I don't care." Mix dragged Julia up from the sofa, spilling the tea from the cup and adding another stain to the cream sofa. "You vultures are all the same."

Julia didn't have time to see how Tia was reacting as Mix launched her down the stairs. She was barely able to catch herself on the handrail.

"Who's Jax?" Julia called back daringly. "You said you saw him before the rehearsal."

"Out!"

Julia didn't need to be asked again. She ducked as a scatter cushion bombed after her. She hesitated at the door, hand on the latch, and listened, but they were still talking in whispers. She gave up on getting anything else from them for now.

Grief could do strange things to people, but tempers like that didn't rise from nowhere. Mix had hardly been a ray of sunshine before Jett's death, but from how she'd painted their relationship with the little she'd offered, Julia could understand why.

Under a blanket of grey clouds, Julia looked to the stage Electric Fury where hadn't got to perform. Dot and Percy were patrolling with their litter pickers. She considered joining them, but she had bigger fish to fry than discarded beer cans and popcorn. Her gaze shifted to the tour bus as it creaked on its axis. She couldn't see much beyond the blackened windows, and the guitar plucking had stopped.

Knocking, she called, "Anyone in?"

The vehicle didn't move another inch.

Maybe the wind had moved it?

"Oi, lady. Have you seen this woman?"

A man in a baseball cap, with a camera slung around his neck, scuttled down the alley holding out a glossy photograph of Mix. Her hair was a natural hue of blonde compared to the bleached white style she had now. Was this back when she was Vivi? From the identification badge around his neck, he was a reporter for the *Daily Razzle*, a paper Julia had never had the misfortune to read.

"I know she's around here somewhere," he whispered, beckoning Julia closer. He pulled a thin roll of purple notes from his pocket. "Hundred quid if you point me in her direction."

It would help towards fixing the café.

"Two hundred."

Would really help.

"Look, I don't have all day. The fact you're even hesitating ... three hundred."

"Must be a big story if you're willing to pay that much." She arched her brow. "Who is she?"

"You been under a rock? Astley-Smythe socialite turned dead rockstar's wife. It's just the sort of stuff our readers drool over. I've had a tip-off from a reliable source, so I know she's around here." He looked around the alley, gazing past the slightly open door of the flat. "Three-fifty, final offer."

The journalist counted out the extra money and wafted it at Julia. She hated how tempted she was. Mix *had* just attempted to throw her down the stairs, after all.

"Never seen her," Julia said, already walking away. "Sorry."

Leaving the reporter to try his hand at getting a response from the tour bus, she joined Barker in his office under the café as the glaziers worked to refit the kitchen window. She filled him in on everything as she made the first notes in her notepad since the quick sketch of Katie's cake.

How she'd love for the right shade of buttercream to be her biggest concern.

"Sounds like the furthest thing from a happy marriage I've ever heard," said Barker, pinning his notes to his quickly filling green felt notice board. "You could press charges for how she threw you out."

"Let's not agitate her too much. She could be innocent."

"I'd say she's our prime suspect."

"Suspects," she said. "Tia interrupted when I asked who set up the rehearsal space. It could be a coincidence, but she seemed rather intent on following along with everything. Now that they know what we're doing, we'll be lucky if either of them says another word."

"They're not the only people who can give us answers."

Remembering Georgia, Julia regretted not using her sacred interview time to ask about Jett's stalker.

"Has Georgia turned up?"

"Not a peep, and I'm not talking about Georgia." He stuck a pin through a website printout on the board. "I've spent all morning trying to find out everything I can about this band. There's little to go on, but I found out who this Jax fella is. He was their drummer until the beginning of this year."

"So, Tia is his replacement?"

"Seems that way." He tapped the black and white picture attached to the small write-up about Jax. "And I can't confirm if he was in the village on the morning of the festival like Mix said, but if he turns up, he's not going to be hard to spot."

Julia couldn't disagree.

"We need to find out more about the band from someone who actually knew them," he said. "Maybe Clive is our next best bet?"

"I'll ask my dad to set something up," she said, eyes narrowing on the pointed spikes of hair jutting from Jax's shaved head. "But until then, I think someone closer to home can help fill in some of these blanks."

8

"*J*essie, if you can hear me, I can't hear you."

Holding the phone higher in the air, Julia left the glow pouring through the post office's shiny new window and walked out onto the squashed grass of the green. Julia's video jittered, but Jessie's side of the call didn't budge from the generic grey icon.

"Can I hear singing?" Jessie's voice broke through. "I read they canned the festival after that guy died?"

"Jett Fury fans," she flipped the camera and pointed it at the church. "They started gathering a few hours ago."

Around a dozen people were as close to the church as possible. Candles flickered among a small mound of flowers and teddies that had been appearing all day. The reporter from the *Daily Razzle* was snapping pictures, but it was the two reporters with camera crews the public mourners were queuing to talk to. Julia had already scanned the sea of dyed black hair, but there was no blue in sight.

"Who even was this guy?"

"Their saviour, apparently." Julia flipped the camera back. "Put your video on."

"Bad signal. Travelling day. Looks like things are evening out there. I saw a mental video of some nutter throwing a flaming bin through the post office window. Is the café okay?"

Julia hesitated.

"Everything's fine," she lied, widening her smile. "Nothing to worry about. It must be the early hours in Tokyo?"

"I'm not in Tokyo." Was she whispering, or was the line that bad? "We've moved on. Got other things to do. Speaking of which, I need to go. I'm about to miss this flight. I'll catch you later, Mum."

Closing her eyes, Julia exhaled.

"I love you."

"You too, Mum. Really have to go now."

Three more months, Julia reminded herself as her reflection stared back at her from the black screen.

She watched her smile fade as the longing to see her daughter started to froth up again.

"You look how I feel," said Shilpa, locking up the post office. "It still doesn't feel real, does it?"

Julia shook her head, not wanting to bring up the real reason behind her visible sadness. Shilpa looked like she'd spent the last two days weeping along with the fans. Another three hopped out of a taxi with more flowers.

"New window," Julia pointed out.

"I still can't believe what happened," Shilpa said with a shake of her head. "I got off lightly compared to your café. Just awful. Do you think his death was an accident?"

"I'm not sure."

"We were right *there*, Julia. We could have saved him."

"How were we to know?"

"He *said* the rug was wet." Shilpa sniffed back hard. "We should have listened. I led him to his death. The greats always die too young."

Julia hoped her friend hadn't spent the two nights since the electrocution coming to that conclusion. Had they missed something that would point to someone's guilt?

"I don't think it was an accident."

"Then I want in." Shilpa batted away her tears, turning to Julia. "If there's any chance of bringing justice to Jett, let me help. I was on my way to help Evelyn with the evening meal at the B&B, but I could spare twenty minutes. What do you need? Say the word."

"This isn't official Peridale's Ears business." Glancing at her gran's cottage, she was glad to see no binoculars at the dark windows. Maybe they were still out litter picking. "I need to know everything *you* know about Jett Fury."

"Everything? I might need longer than twenty minutes."

"Make sure you use *real* milk. Julia tried to fob me off with something rotten the other morning." Dot's voice floated up from the basement as Julia held open the door for Shilpa. "I told Percy, you always make sure you have some long life in the..." Her voice drifted off as they walked down the wooden stairs into the dark office. "Shilpa? What are you doing here?"

"Shilpa is our resident Jett Fury expert," Julia said, ducking into the basement. "Her insight is going to be invaluable. Gran, what are *you* doing here?"

"Nothing gets past me in this village, dear." She fluffed up her curls behind her ears. "I've had a cursory glance over your notes. I have thoughts. Barker, are these your only biscuits?"

Glaring down at the packet of plain digestives, Dot plucked one out before planting herself in the leather swivel chair behind Barker's mahogany desk in the centre of the room.

"She *always* serves digestives," Barker whispered to Julia as she put together her cup of peppermint and liquorice. "So much for a secret. I did try to get rid of her."

"She'll keep us on our toes."

With her tea and biscuits, Julia and Shilpa took the leather sofa. No amount of subtle throat clearing moved Dot from Barker's chair, so he sat on the other side of the desk where clients usually did.

"You have *five* suspects?" said Dot, putting her feet up on the corner of the desk. "Mix, the wife, I definitely understand. The manager, Clive, I could understand. The blue-haired girl seems like a piece of work, and I don't know who Tia or Jax are."

"Tia is their new drummer as of this festival season," Shilpa said, pulling apart the sari around her neck to show a black t-shirt with a silver metallic Electric Fury logo printed across a fireball. "It's where I got this. We all thought she was good, but it's not the same without Jax."

"Jax is the former drummer," Barker explained,

pointing to the printed web page. "Real name *was* Jason Robertson. Changed it to Jax Star in 2000."

"That's when I first saw them live," Shilpa said, looking at Julia. "I met my husband, Gerald, at college a few years before that, and he was really into gigs back then, as shy as he was. My parents forbade me from going, and they were never my thing, but I was so besotted by Gerald that I would have followed him anywhere. The live music thing didn't really click for me until he took me to an Electric Fury show. Original line-up back then. They said it was their first show, and it was only a tiny bar as big as this room." Smiling at the memory, she looked down at her hand. "He proposed to me outside the theatre that night. My parents forbade me from marrying him too, but I was already in love."

"Shilpa, that's rather sweet." Dot helped herself to another biscuit. "How come we barely see your husband? Not killed him off and buried him under the conservatory, have you?"

"Gran!"

"Some of us commute in, Dorothy," Shilpa said with a glare. "And my Gerald is a very busy man, I'll have you know. Works for the council, and before you ask, he had no idea about the festival. Where was I?"

"First Electric Fury show," said Barker.

"Ah, yes." She dunked a biscuit in her tea. "They

were fantastic, though Gerald admitted many years later that he'd only taken me to that show to try and impress me. Wanted me to think he was cool. He's always preferred the opera, which sends me to sleep."

"These three original members?" said Julia. "Jett, Jax, and..."

"Gef with a G."

"Gef?" Dot laughed. "Hardly rockstar material."

"It was his real name. They were three friends when they decided to start a band. Think they decided over a drink one night. I can't quite remember the story of what happened to Gef, but he was their bassist until Mix took over around 2011."

"Seeing as they're no strangers to line-up changes, it makes a little more sense that Mix and Tia would carry on without them," Julia was scribbling down the information. "Having no original members never stopped the Sugababes."

"Or The Supremes," said Dot.

"And Thin Lizzy," added Barker, though none of them nodded. "Just me? Shilpa, do you know why Jax left?"

"Their last show together was just before Christmas at a theatre over in Cheltenham." She sipped her tea before putting it on the floor next to her. "I used to keep up with their newsletter more, but

I've been so busy lately, what with the post office and the neighbourhood watch—"

"You've missed the last two official meetings," Dot pointed out. "But do carry on. What else do you know about them?"

Leaving her tea on the floor, Shilpa walked over to the board and scanned the notes Barker had been organising into columns. She tapped one of the notes under 'THE BAND'.

"I can answer this one," she said. "They don't record their music, so that's why they don't have vinyl."

"That's been puzzling me," he said. "What sort of band doesn't record music?"

"A bad one," said Dot. "I watched some videos on the internet of them at other shows, and I don't see all the fuss. Just some ageing rockstar with a whiny voice. I've seen better-looking people on the number six bus."

"It wasn't about his looks," Shilpa said softly. "It's about his *songs*. His way with words was special, and his voice was like honey and smoke. People went to their shows *because* they were a live-only group. Jett always made sure to point it out at every gig. The only way to experience their music outside of videos people recorded was to see them live."

"So, a gimmick?" Dot joined her at the board. "A

word-of-mouth experience. I used to go to a bingo hall that didn't advertise."

Julia finished scribbling and stuck the note to the board.

"This Georgia?" Julia asked, tapping the blank space under the note detailing her readiness to commit theft. "Do you know anything about her? Did Jett Fury mention that he had a crazy fan with a restraining order who might want to kill him?"

"First I heard of that was when he said it in the alley," Shilpa said, looking through the wall. "I still can't believe I stood so close to him, so soon before he..."

Julia plucked a tissue from the box on the desk, and Shilpa scooped it up immediately, turning away from them.

"Who has the most to gain from Jett being dead?" Dot took her turn at the wall, her finger tapping against the side of her face. "Like I said, Mix and Clive are the most likely suspects. Their columns say it all."

"They're the ones we've had the most experiences with," Barker pointed out. "Don't let quantity sway your bias. But you're right. Mix, at least, has the most solid motive in my eyes. She sounds like a live wire ... if you'll pardon the pun. Shilpa, know anything about her?"

"Mix?" Shilpa turned back, scrunching up the tissue. "You don't know who she is?"

"She said her real name," Julia clicked her fingers. "Vivi?"

"Vivienne Astley-Smythe," said Shilpa. "Her father is Astor Astley-Smythe. He's some Lord of somewhere, and from what I've heard, owns more land than anyone should."

"So, she's from deep pockets money?" said Julia, understanding why the reporter had been so eager to get the scoop. "And yet she said she didn't have much choice but to carry on with the band."

"They must have cut her off," said Dot certainly. "The rich can be so cruel."

"She's more famous than him depending on which message board you go on," said Shilpa. "Jett would sometimes bring it up at shows. I always thought it made her look uncomfortable, but she'd laugh." Frowning, she added, "I suppose she *was* on stage with everyone looking at her."

"True British aristocracy, according to this article." Barker's phone lit up his face in the dim basement. "We need to talk to her again. This gets more interesting by the—"

"I need to go!" Shilpa winced at her watch before gulping down the rest of her tea. "I promised Evelyn I'd help with the evening meal. They all paid upfront for the weekend, so she's still got a full house until tomorrow."

"Then let's get a move on!" Dot announced. "You know what Evelyn is like. Georgia might still be there."

"Play nice, Gran."

"I'm always nice, dear," she said. "But I'd bet my pension Georgia is hiding there. It wouldn't be the first time Evelyn's misguided kindness prompted her to hide a criminal, would it? With any luck, that bonkers girl with the batty blue hair is there and still has your money."

9

$\mathcal{A}$fter three tugs of the musical doorbell, Evelyn finally answered the bustling bed and breakfast's door. Like the village on the morning of the festival, Julia had never seen the place so busy.

"Where is she?" Dot asked the moment they were over the threshold. "No funny business."

"If you could be more specific? I'm a little busy."

"You're the psychic. You tell me."

Julia nudged Dot in the ribs with her elbow, but Evelyn closed her eyes. While she searched the stars for the answer, Julia peeked into the dining room. There wasn't an empty chair as people waited for their evening meal. From the number of guests checking their watches, they'd come to help at the right time. No blue hair in sight, though.

"Georgia!" Evelyn clicked her fingers together. "And no, she's not here, and I'm not hiding her, and I don't have a lick of time to stand here talking about it."

Evelyn hurried off with Shilpa hot on her heels, leaving Dot to peek her head under the stairs.

"Just making sure," she said to Julia's arched brow. "How did she know?"

"Psychic, remember?" Julia couldn't contain her smile at her gran's befuddled expression. "C'mon, let's make ourselves useful while we're here. Looks like she could use all the hands she can get."

In the small kitchen at the back of the B&B, plates waiting to be filled covered every inch of the counter space. A flurry of steam burst from the oven as Evelyn pulled out a dish of something topped with roasted aubergine slices. She swapped it for an unbaked version, passing the cooked one into Shilpa's oven mitts.

Julia washed her hands at the sink, surprised to see a dozen tents lining the garden's lawns under a blanket of twinkling string lanterns.

"My grandson's idea," said Evelyn, draining some oil into the sink. "Even with the No Vacancies sign, they kept showing up, and I didn't have the heart to turn them away. You might find some answers in that bottom tent."

"Ha!" Dot snapped upright, pulling her head from the cupboards she'd been checking. "She *is* here!"

"By all of the stars in the sky, Dorothy, I wouldn't lie to you." Evelyn rushed past and joined Shilpa in scooping. "She came alone last week, and the girl scarcely left her room, but a friend of hers turned up for the festival, and he's barely left his tent either. I can sense that he's in there." Julia glanced to the bottom tent, which was emitting a soft glow. "Can't you see I have enough to deal with without your allegations? The police have already searched the place from top to bottom. She's not here. If you're not going to help me feed the five thousand, make some room, please."

"Alright, Evelyn." Dot backed down, joining Julia at the window. "Keep your turban on. I was only making sure. The girl's probably a murderer."

"We don't know that yet, Gran,"

"She's only a child," said Evelyn. "Though her aura was a worrisome shade of black for someone so young. But a child nonetheless."

"A *fanatical* child. No offence, Shilpa."

"Excuse you, I'm not *fanatical*."

"Julia?" Evelyn cut through before the bickering started. "Do you think she killed that poor man?"

"I'm not sure," Julia said. "I saw her scale a fence like it was nothing. And that was after she mugged my father, a man twice her size. *And* she did all that after breaking into Jessie's flat. Jett did have a restraining order against her."

"And you just admitted that she's been in the village all week," said Dot, pulling open the back door. "Planning Jett's murder up in her room, no doubt. Now, should I lead this one?"

"I think I've got it, Gran."

"Only if you're sure?"

"Positive."

"Then where do you want me, Evelyn? I suppose I should make myself useful."

Leaving them in the kitchen, Julia walked down the garden path separating the two rows of tents. A chill had fallen now that the sun was almost finished setting. The tents mainly looked unoccupied, making the light within the tent nearest the shed at the bottom stand out. Glancing at the single pair of men's trainers outside, Julia gave the polyester an awkward knock.

"Georgia?" There was a frantic scramble at the zip. He ripped it down before zipping it back almost all the way. "Who are you?"

"I'm looking for Georgia," she said, crouching and offering a soft smile to the teenage face peering out at her. "I think we met yesterday at the festival. I'm Julia."

"No, we didn't."

"Popcorn?" she said, shuffling closer. "You tried to buy a bottle of prosecco and pink sambuca?"

"I don't remember," he said, letting the zip down more. "But that sounds like something I'd try to do. It's been a strange weekend. Kieran."

"For you and me both." She held out her hand, but he only stared at it. "Nice to formally meet you, Kieran."

"What do you want?"

"I'm going to assume Georgia isn't in?"

"She's been gone for two days," he said. "Haven't seen her since the first day."

"Did you hear about what happened at the church?"

"I've been in a tent, not under a rock." He bit before quickly adding, "Sorry. Like I said, weird weekend."

"I won't hold it against you." She winked, glad to see a smile from him. "Georgia was with you when you bought popcorn from my café. Don't suppose you remember when exactly you last saw her? It's rather important."

"Festival fog. I don't remember much after waking up here on Saturday morning. She's always wandering off."

"Have you reported her disappearance to the police?"

"Been friends with Georgia since we were little, and she's *always* come back by now."

Kieran stared off through the tent, and Julia could easily imagine how much of the past few days he'd spent hoping every sound was his friend's return. Constant worrying, but not enough to have reported her as missing.

"She's been in touch," Julia stated.

"A couple of texts," he admitted in a whisper. "But she's being weird. Weirder than usual. And she's posting online like crazy, non-stop."

"Posting?" Julia moved in closer. "What's her username?"

Kieran's eyes narrowed on her.

"Would her posts have anything to do with Jett Fury?"

"How do you know about that? *I'm* her best friend, and she barely talks to me about it. I'd never have come if I'd known Electric Fury were headlining, but she booked everything. Who says no to a free festival? Now I wish I hadn't bothered."

"You arrived on Friday?" she asked, to which he nodded. "Do you know why Georgia came five days earlier?"

"She follows Jett around," he said in a whisper.

"It's super weird, but when they post where they're going to be playing, she goes there. Usually sleeps rough, but this B&B is cheap as chips."

"That can't be easy. Doesn't she worry people by being gone for so long at her age?"

"No one to worry except for me these days."

Is that why Georgia had latched onto the band?

"Do you know what she did to get a restraining order against her?"

"Restraining order?" Kieran's cheeks flushed a deep red. "You're not joking, are you? I *knew* I should have stayed at home. She never used to be like this, but then her mum died. Georgia ran up on stage during their set at a festival in York three days later, and she's been acting nutty ever since. She swore she wouldn't do it again, but she broke onto his tour bus in Sheffield a few days after that and…"

"And what?"

"She set it on fire."

"Oh."

"Like I said … nutty."

"Don't suppose she brought back a wad of cash at any point? She made off with my popcorn takings after breaking into the place where Jett was staying."

"I haven't seen her."

If he was lying, Julia couldn't catch him out.

"Can you call her?" Julia nodded at the phone

charging from a power bank in the corner. "Ask her where she is?"

"Like I said, only texts." His eyes narrowed on Julia. "That's just Georgia. Who did you say you were, again? A popcorn seller?"

"My granddaughter is many things," Dot announced her arrival halfway up the garden path. "A member of Peridale's Ears Neighbourhood Watch for one, and we are here investigating the murder of Jett Fury."

"Gran..."

"Georgia didn't do it." Kieran reached for the zip and yanked it up halfway. "She wouldn't. She's had it hard, okay? She does those things because she *loves* him, not because..."

He stared down at the grass, and Julia wondered if he was starting to see the picture the way she was; how Jett would have, on the other side of the invasion.

"I don't know where she is, alright."

Kieran dragged the zip around, and the light went off inside. Dot gave the door a knock, but Julia pulled her back.

"I think he told me everything he knows," she said, looking off to the last streaks of pink peppering the horizon. "She has a habit of wandering off and doing strange things."

"Wandering off and killing, no doubt."

Julia wanted to disagree and believe that the young girl was misguided and innocent in her obsession but hearing how far she'd gone with the tour bus stopped her.

"If she *did* kill him and had any sense," said Dot as they walked back towards the B&B's back door, "she'd be on the other side of the world like Jessie by now, and your money probably helped get her there."

Back at the kitchen window, looking out at the rows of tents as Kieran's head scanned through a small gap, Julia couldn't deny her grandmother's conclusion sounded plausible. Whether Georgia had killed her beloved Jett Fury or not, Julia couldn't imagine the girl missing the fallout.

But if Georgia hadn't run to her best friend, where had she gone?

10

In the months Julia had attended the baby music classes at the village hall, the noise had never bothered her as much as it did the following afternoon. Wincing, she smiled at Olivia, who was having the time of her life smacking a tambourine. With the other twenty or so babies and toddlers hitting drums, pounding xylophones, and shaking maracas, the cacophony was almost as bad as the Electric Fury performance Barker had been listening to in the bath the night before.

"And then I said to him," Katie said, leading Vinnie out of the village hall after the class, "if he didn't go to bed soon, he was never going to wake up to go chasing that 18th-century armoire he's been obsessing about all week. But you know what your father is like when he gets on the whisky. Can't stop him from talking the night away. I'm just glad I wasn't the one whose ear he was chewing off. I thought sitting down all day would be easier than running around the café, but back-to-back nail clients are more of a workout than I imagined. I'm going to have arms like that Jane Fonda if I... Not boring you, am I, Julia?"

Julia snapped away from staring at the doors of St. Peter's Church on their way to the gates. The police had gone, and yet the doors were still closed. She pulled herself away from wondering if looking at the place where Jett died would help ease her thoughts.

"Sorry, million miles away."

"You were somewhere else that whole time."

"I'm here." She pushed forward a smile. "And that sounds like my father. Whose ear was he chewing off if not yours?"

"What's his face?" Katie clicked her keys, and her baby pink Fiat 500 blipped to life on the edge of the village green. "Clyde?"

"Clive Winston?"

"That's him. An old friend from way back when." She bent over to strap Vinnie into his car seat. "And it must be from way back when because he's never mentioned him. You'd never know, given that they were getting on like a house on fire. Reminiscing about all the antiques your father used to source for him for his big house out in the country. On and on and on. I had to go to bed." She slammed the door and looked out to the café. "Is it as awful as Dot said?"

"For once, she might not have been embellishing."

"Such a pointless shame." Katie opened the passenger door and forced Julia in, with Olivia clutched to her chest. "I don't have anyone booked in for another half an hour. You need pampering, and I'm not taking no for an answer."

Julia had intended to take another stab at talking to Mix or Tia, but she didn't argue, and halfway through Katie's foot massage in a reclining chair in the salon, she was glad she hadn't.

"Can you imagine being electrocuted?" Katie shuddered, putting her back into rubbing away the knots in Julia's sole. "How could something like that happen?"

"That's what I'm trying to figure out," Julia said, almost to herself, suddenly wanting to pull her feet away at the thought of what happened. "I don't suppose you overheard Clive talking about what happened? I've been meaning to speak to him. If I'd known he was at yours, I might have joined you for a tipple."

"I wasn't really paying much attention."

"Oh."

"He said the girls were keen to continue the band," she said, switching from massaging to scrubbing her heels with something that resembled a cheese grater. "Think he might have said he'd found a replacement for the one who got zapped. Ah, that'll be my next appointment. She's early."

Leaving Julia at the back of the salon, Katie hurried to her neon reception desk. Clive must work quickly if he'd found someone to replace Jett only three days after he "got zapped". She pulled out her notepad and scribbled down the detail, but a squeal from Katie made her twist in her chair before she could think about it any further. She was jumping up and down with a less than willing white-haired participant. Over Katie's shoulder, Mix stared ahead at Julia.

"Seems I can't get away from you," she said as Katie let her go.

"You two know each other?" inquired Katie.

"No." Mix shrugged off her fur coat and handed it to Katie to hang up as she assessed the place. "I can't believe you've got your own business. Should have known from the shockingly pink flyer that came through the door this morning that you were Katie. Your father cut *you* off too?"

"Died and left me with the debt."

"That old chestnut." Mix slumped down into the chair behind the nail desk. "You got anything to drink?"

"Tea or coffee?"

"Anything stronger?" She picked up a bottle of nail varnish remover. "The police have been pecking my skull all morning."

"Any news?" Julia left the notepad on the chair arm and walked over. "Looks like they're finished in the church."

"Julia South-Brown," Mix stated with a sigh, finally making eye contact. Without her heavy black eye makeup, she looked much younger. "With the ex-DI-turned-PI husband, neighbourhood watch nanna, and penchant for do-goodery and snoopery. You've got quite the reputation around here."

"Given how things circulate, I'd say only half of it was true. You two know each other?"

"What's it to you?"

"Vivi, this is my stepdaughter." Katie rubbed a cotton swab against the first chipped fingernail. "I'm married to her father."

"It's Mix these days." She looked Julia up and down. "And *I* thought it was weird that *my* parents are technically cousins. These small villages really are a hoot. Must be a dinosaur. Hope he's rich."

"He ... tries." Katie nodded for Julia to pull up a

chair, prompting a sigh from Mix. "And we go way back, don't we? Regular old party girls back in our day. Where did we meet again? Was it a gala or a ball?"

"Those years are a blur."

"You were always drinking champagne on the tables." Katie giggled. "Remember when you stole that man's horse that kicked in his Aston Martin's back window?

"Like I said, a blur."

"How do you two know each other?" Katie asked.

"Julia turned up pretending to be a concerned local with free food so she could covertly ask me questions," Mix said, sucking her teeth. "Or something like that."

"And then Mix threw me down the stairs."

"Which practically makes us the best of friends." Mix's phone, which she'd put on the desk next to her, started vibrating. It was Clive, and there was an emoji of a pig next to his name. "Not a bad cook, I'll give you that. Beats the takeaways around here, at least."

The phone continued to ring, and Mix continued to ignore it.

"Band trouble?"

"Jax trouble," she muttered. "The man *cannot* sing. Clive has been driving me up the wall sending demos all morning, hence why I needed to get out of the flat.

We're well and truly doomed. I will never be able to show my face in public again, which might be for the best. The police still won't let me leave this hell hole. Given their clear incompetence, I might still be here when your travelling daughter returns at Christmas. Funny what information people in these places will volunteer without you even asking."

"She's in Japan, right, Julia?"

"Oh, I'm not sure. She was on the move yesterday."

Reaching out for the polishes lined up on the walls, Katie plucked out black.

"No," said Mix. "Anything but black. They've been black for years. Jett insisted."

"Since 2011, right?" said Julia.

"So, I'm not the only one who did my research." Mix smiled, raising her brows. "Gef was already on his way out when I met Jett at that hunter's ball. Gef wanted to settle down. A real job and kids didn't really mesh with the rockstar lifestyle."

"They were old friends, weren't they? Came up with the idea in a pub?"

"You've read their website, then." Mix laughed. "That's the official story, but it's codswallop. Jett made up their origin story to appeal to the common man. He knew the type of gigs he'd get. He didn't think telling people that he put an ad in the paper and they were the only two that auditioned really worked. Gef was a total *yes* man until he dipped out. I think that's why Jett kept me around. He wasn't used to people who spoke their minds. Rubbed him the wrong way, but he liked that sometimes."

She was livelier than she'd been in the flat. Was that for Katie's benefit, or was she already getting over what happened?

"And Jax?" Julia pushed. "Another yes man?"

"Not if you asked him." A bitter laugh this time. "Jett kept him around for so long because Jax would always bow down to whatever Jett wanted, but last year, something flipped in Jax. I think he got sick and tired of bowing down and started pushing back over every detail. But even when he was trying to stand up to Jett, he was still a spineless, sniffling, sack of—"

"How about a lovely turquoise?" Katie called loudly, nodding to Olivia and Vinnie in their small playpen in the corner. "Would go lovely with your complexion."

"What sorts of things did Jax push for?" Julia asked, glad Mix was being forthcoming.

"Never anything ever worthwhile. He'd argue for three weeks about a single word in a lyric or what colour he was allowed to dye his hair. Jett always got the final say, as per the contracts. Drove Jax crazy. Then one day, a huge row, and bye-bye Jax and hello

Tia. I don't think Jax ever thought Jett would get around to it. Took him long enough to adjust when Gef left. And now we're without any of them. Clive's plan for us to keep going better work. Otherwise, I can't afford the therapy from the years of hell they've put me through."

The veil of mystery around Mix continued to lift. With controlling parents and a band full of manchildren, no wonder Mix had a simmering rage that seemed likely to burst out at the end of every sentence.

"Has Clive worked with the band for long?"

"A few years," she said with a vague tilting of her head. "Promised Jett he'd take us to the next level. To his credit, we've been performing on bigger stages every festival season since. This was our first headlining spot. People don't really come out to see specific bands, but festivals are great for hoovering up new fans for our solo shows. That's all Jett cared about. I don't think Jax liked that he wasn't going to be part of our biggest show yet – not that we got there."

"Jett didn't seem all that excited."

"That was just Jett," she said with a shrug. "Too cool for school."

"And did he always perform barefoot?"

"Every time. Said it was the only way he could feel connected. He went to one Buddhist retreat six years ago, and not wearing shoes was the only thing he picked up."

'Every time' meant all the suspects would have known he'd be barefoot on the wet patch. It didn't rule anyone out, but it strengthened the idea that Jett's death wasn't an accident.

"You said you saw Jax that day," said Julia, trying the question she'd called up the stairs after being thrown out. "Jett seemed to think you were saying it to wind him up."

"I was. Petty, I know, but those moments felt like victories over him."

"Did you speak with Jax?"

Without missing a beat, Mix said, "No. And now he's back in the band. I have no desire to say two words to the man after listening to his pathetic attempts at emulating Jett. Those record labels would be idiots to sign us now. He's nothing but a bad backup singer, but he grew up with a dad who sold fruit and veg at Camden Market. He can talk the talk, but that's as far as it goes. Probably told Clive he could just pick up Jett's guitar, and *voila*! Electric Fury 4.0 is born. The crowds will eat him alive."

"Given all the stuff left outside the church," said Katie as she finished painting Mix's nails, "you have enough fans that it might work?"

"Jett made sure they were all his. He wasn't very

good at sharing the spotlight. Literally. We'd be lucky if he even had the technicians light us at most shows."

"Why not be a solo act if he loved all the attention?"

"He was," she said. "Before he was Jett Fury, he was Jamie C. Signed a bad deal in the nineties, and they forced him into bubble-gum pop with the choreography to match. He looked a prize fool, and it didn't work. Peaked at seventy-six on the charts. He went bankrupt buying himself out of the contract, and then Electric Fury was born. After that, he never signed a contract he didn't write himself. And boy, did that man love a contract. He was terrified of signing his life away again."

"Is that why you're a live-only band?"

"Sounds silly, doesn't it?" Mix laughed. "I always said we should record, but it always had to be on his terms. Labels have been trying to get him to record the music for years, but he's never been interested. Part of me wondered if he was worried he couldn't take the electricity from the stage to the booth."

Mix paused and frowned, perhaps at her word choice.

"Maybe it's best to leave it all behind," she continued. "Give up and crawl back to Mother and Father before I'm as old as the audience looking up at me."

"The band has young fans too. Like a girl with blue hair?"

"So, you've met Georgia?" Mix gritted her teeth. "Blue hair, green hair, pink hair. Different place, different colour. Jett did say she was here, but he's been saying that at every stop on this tour, and I've only seen her half of those times."

"Do you know why she was so obsessed?"

"Does it matter? They *thought* they knew him. They didn't know the first thing. You know he hated the sight of blood? And the dark. And he was scared of dogs. But to them, he was everything they needed him to be. The rockstar they couldn't be. He'd love all the attention they're giving him now if he was still—" Twisted in her chair, Mix glared through the window. "Oh, not him again."

The reporter from the *Daily Razzle* exited a boutique across the street. He looked up and down, glancing at the neon sign, but not into the shop.

"Someone keeps tipping off reporters about my whereabouts." She pulled her hands away and hurried to her fur coat. "If it's Clive, I'll wring his neck. He's been trying to get me to do a sit-down sob-story interview to promote our comeback. Have you got a back door I can sneak out of? I'd rather talk to my parents than those slimeballs."

"They're not dry."

"Already smudged." Mix apologised with a smile as she pulled on her coat. "Sorry, Katie. Really great to see you." Fluffing out her hair, she turned to Julia. "Given your questioning, you think it was murder, don't you?"

"Don't you?"

"Who knows." Mix followed Katie to the back of the shop, tripping over the edge of the playpen on the way. Vinnie laughed, but Olivia burst out crying at the interruption. Mix fell into the chair Julia had been sitting in for her foot massage. "Sorry, I should lay off the wine with breakfast, but being a widow will do that to you. So, Julia, who do you think did it?"

Was she checking to see if Julia was going to say her?

"I'd really like to talk to Georgia," Julia said, choosing her words carefully. "And Jax, now that I know he's around."

Turning to face Julia at the open back door, Mix's eyes were too busy looking at the window as a second reporter stalked the streets of Mulberry Lane.

"You're not so bad," said Mix, pulling sunglasses from her pocket before jamming them on. "Maybe these small villages aren't the worst places to end up. We might become neighbours if Jax doesn't learn how to sing before the end of the week. At least it's quiet. Almost like paradise, don't you think?"

"Paradise enough for me," Julia said, following her to the alley that backed up against a row of cottages. "Same question to you. Who do *you* think did it?"

"I never said I thought it was murder."

"But if you did?"

"I don't know," she said, already hurrying off. "But doesn't it seem like Jax just got everything he ever wanted?"

Back in the salon, Katie brought out the remaining nail varnish cake, still half intact.

"And can you believe I thought this was a bad omen," she said, ripping the marzipan label in half before cramming it into her mouth. "You'll never believe how much I made on that festival day. Almost makes me wish they'd waited until the end of the festival to bump him off."

"Looking at what happened to my café, maybe the omen wasn't for you." Julia ran her finger along the crusted pink buttercream. "Is Mix like you remember?"

"I don't remember Vivi being so sad. She was always the life of the party, but we were all a lot younger back then. I was already drifting away from the scene when she was in the heat of it. Do you think she could have killed him? My father used to say there's power in a well-timed exit, and she seemed pretty set on having the idea of Jax killing Jett be the last thing on your mind."

"Excellent point, Katie." Julia sucked the buttercream from her fingers, which was as sweet as she remembered. "Excellent point indeed."

11

_J_ulia left the salon with Olivia through the back door after watching two more men with cameras rush up and down Mulberry Lane, searching for Mix. Before she'd left, Katie had suggested that Mix could have called the paparazzi herself, something the socialites she used to hang around with back in the day would often do when leaving nightclubs. Half wanted to become famous for being famous, and the other half just wanted to annoy their parents. Mix could have fit into either category – not that Katie could remember Mix specifically doing such a thing.

Given how hard Mix was trying to evade them, Julia wasn't sure that was what was happening. Mix had accused Clive of calling them in the name of promotion, which seemed far more likely.

Walking back towards the village green with Olivia, Julia went over everything Mix had said before the paparazzi showed up. She'd been far more willing to open up about her time in the band. She also hadn't tried to keep secret how petty she could be towards Jett in the name of getting her own back against his apparent mistreatment of her. There seemed to be little love remaining between the couple in their final days together.

But was Mix behind Jett's electrocution?

Mix had a temper and didn't mind showing it, but Jett's death wasn't the result of a quick temper. That much was clear. If Mix had wanted Jett out of the way, she'd have had access to him every day. She could have slipped poison into his food, or smothered him with a pillow. If she'd really wanted to electrocute him, a plugged-in hairdryer thrown into the shower would have done it.

What happened at the church was far more calculated.

From the suspects, Jax and Georgia were the only ones without proper access to Jett, not that Georgia wasn't constantly trying. Julia reached into her bag for her notepad to write down her thoughts.

It wasn't there.

"Chair arm," Julia thought aloud, looking back towards Mulberry Lane as they passed The Plough pub. "We'll go back for it later. What do you say?" She sniffed. "I'd say it's time that you need a nappy change, Miss Stinky."

Like she could see her notepad resting on the chair arm at the back of the salon, Julia could see the changing bag kept in the cupboard in the café. She walked up to the door and unlocked it without a second thought. Too used to not working on Mondays these days, the door swung open to remind her that this time, her maternity leave wasn't behind her absence.

Head down, Julia hurried into the kitchen and retrieved the bag from the cupboard, which the vandals hadn't pulled open. After freshening up Olivia, she stood behind the counter and looked out at the café, just like she had done a week ago on her first day back.

There were no tables to have neat sugar pots on, and the blind was down so the sun couldn't break through in pretty lines. The pictures of Peridale were gone, and the broken display cabinets dragged into the yard to await collection for repair. The vandals had even dragged what looked like keys across the counter.

"What a difference a week makes, hmm?" she said

brightly to Olivia, who was happily oblivious to the destruction around them. "Should we go home to see what Daddy is…"

Julia's voice trailed off as her eyes drifted to the wall of postcards. She hadn't given the cards a second thought in the hurry to sweep up the glass and clear out the wood. Maybe they'd been too stuck under the layer of spray paint to notice. Putting Olivia down on the tiles, she unhooked the string and peeled the cards back.

All of the beautiful pictures Jessie had selected were gone. The spray paint scribbles were as much a part of their story now as the messages on the back. There was some bleeding around the edges, but her words were at least still there. She turned the most recent one from Japan and read over it again.

'Miss you all a million! Can't wait to see you all soon.'

Like ghosts from a time gone by, Julia could see the two of them whizzing about the place in her mind's eye. Jessie had started as an apprentice at sixteen, eager to learn and prove herself, and by the time she left to see the world at nineteen, she could run the café as well as Julia could on her best day. Like two performers in the circus, they'd been able to juggle anything by each other's side, always having each other's back, always knowing what the other needed. An unstoppable force held together by their love and trust for each other.

For once, she didn't want Jessie there with her.

Not with their café in this state.

Placing the ruined cards in a stack, she looked around for somewhere to keep them safe. Crouching, she dug among the storage boxes under the counter. She pushed her account files to the side and smiled at seeing an old shoe box covered in floral wrapping paper.

"Put your first of everything in here," her gran had said when she'd handed her the box on opening day. "No matter how trivial. You'll want these memories one day."

Knowing there was no better place, Julia pulled out the box and blew off a layer of dust. She pulled off the lid to see Jessie's first wage slip sitting on top. It wasn't the final first by a long stretch, but from that moment, she'd been too busy living her dream to keep cataloguing it the same way. Digging past the first invoices and receipts and even the first used sugar packets and flour bags, her fingers brushed against the metal framed picture waiting for her at the bottom.

Another gift from her gran.

A frenzied knock at the door pulled her fingers away.

"Sorry, we're closed."

"Tour bus is blocked up, and I'm bursting." A man with incredibly pointed hair ducked into the café, legs half-crossed. "Please?"

"Absolutely." Julia's face lit up as she pointed to the door. "My pleasure."

Barker had been right about not being able to miss Jax. She'd have seen the neon green spikes jutting from his shaved head from a great distance even through a thick fog. Julia stuffed the postcards in the box and replaced the lid, smiling as though her café wasn't a total wasteland.

"I can't offer you a slice of cake, but how about a tea or coffee on the house?" she offered as Jax emerged, patting the drinks machine. "One of the few things the vandals didn't get around to smashing."

He took in the café as though he hadn't noticed the graffiti on his rush in. "I'll pass."

Jax left, but Julia wasn't going to waste her opportunity. After running Olivia across to Dot and Percy, who were more than happy to sort out Olivia's lunch, Julia wasted no time making her way to the tour bus. Walking down the alley, she wondered if Jax had been the one on board when her knock had gone unanswered. If he'd been in the village on the day of Jett's death, she couldn't imagine he'd gone very far in the meantime.

Knuckles clenched and outstretched, she walked towards the van parked behind the post office. Cigar smoke came from the other side, closer to her café. She hopped back, peeking around to see Clive and Jax leaning against the wooden fence. Clive was puffing as usual, and Jax was wafting it away. Heads low, they might have been looking out as the festival crew dismantled the stage, but Julia was sure they were exchanging words. She'd seen enough people hunched over in her café to know the more they tried to make it look like they weren't arguing, the tenser they became.

"Is that you, Julia?"

The familiar sound of her father's voice came from inside the tour bus. She couldn't see him behind the blackened windows, but she could hear his footsteps as the bus rocked like it had when she'd been ignored. Someone had definitely been on board. Her father appeared at the door with a grin as wide as his open shirt collar. He looked to be in one of his finest suits.

"Don't look so worried. I was invited onboard." He leaned out and looked in Clive and Jax's direction. They hadn't moved, though Clive's hands had expressively joined in with his straining shoulders. "Clive's had me running around every antique shop in the Cotswolds for the *perfect* chair."

"A chair is his most pressing concern right now?"

"One of many." He motioned for her to follow him on the bus. "It's been a busy morning. You'll never guess what we've been doing."

"Recording music?"

"How did you know?"

"Evelyn's rubbing off on me."

Julia had imagined the tour bus would feel more significant on the inside, but the opposite was true. Behind the front cabin, separated by a metal wall with a hatch, were two rows of seats with a table in the middle, a small kitchenette, and a slender cupboard door behind which she imagined the blocked toilet must be. The back of the bus was taken up by a bright white recording booth, the only thing on board that looked remotely new. The freshness of the paint only made the burn marks around the edges stand out all the more. No wonder the band hadn't wanted to stay on the bus.

"Pretty swish, eh?" He patted the seat next to him and picked up one of many bottles. "Champagne?"

"If I didn't know any better, I'd say Clive is rubbing off on you." Julia accepted a glass after he sloshed some out. She took a sip. "Is it supposed to taste like that?"

"It's not the best," her father said, pouring himself a top-up. "But it's champagne all the same. You can't blame Clive for going for the cheap stuff with all Jax's demands. Not that Jax will touch the stuff. Probably not good enough for him. He's been in that booth all morning, trying to get the perfect take. It's all been very rock'n'roll. I could have been a singer, you know."

He crooned in her ear, cigars on his breath with the champagne.

"I hope you've been paying attention to their discussion. I've been meaning to talk to you about Clive." She scooped the glass from her father, more than sure he'd had enough. "Why has he had you running around after a chair?"

"For my new star, that's why!" Clive heaved himself into the bus. "And what is it you want to talk about?"

"Oh, Julia can cater for the shoot!" Brian clicked his fingers together, his knees jolting the table. "You can put on a buffet tomorrow, can't you, love? I'm sure there's room in the budget, right, Clive?"

Jax followed Clive on board and rushed over as Brian knocked the table again, clunking the champagne flutes together. "Careful! My vision must be protected."

"Oops." Brian hiccupped. "It's been a long day."

It was barely past noon.

"Vision?" she asked.

"That's what the chair is for," said Brian. "Jax has had a vision for a music video."

"And you're filming it tomorrow?"

"That's show business." Clive checked his watch. "We only have the rest of the week to pull something together for the showcase if we're going to save this band from fading into obscurity, speaking of which, flower, if you would…" He propped the door open, and Julia knew it was for her. "Unless you can provide me with a location to shoot this flick, I'm going to ask you to exit the tour bus. Another cigar, Brian?"

Arm still holding open the door, he patted in his pocket before tossing one at the couch.

"I'll be across soon," he said, the cigar already between his lips. "Don't tell your grandmother. Or Katie. Or your sister. In fact, pretend you've seen nothing."

Julia walked to the door, and Clive's arm didn't move. She wondered if he didn't want her to leave for a moment, but he'd made that quite clear.

"I'm not going to crouch under it."

"Quite right," he said, bowing his head and offering her the door. "Would you like a red carpet too? I'll let you know about the catering after we've discussed our options."

The door slammed behind Julia the second her foot touched the path. Jax was crouched on the step behind the café's yard door. He was going through the papers he'd salvaged, grunting as he shook out the wet ones.

"I'm going to have to do all this again," he said when he noticed Julia looking. "You're the woman with the toilet."

"I do have one of those, yes." She looked down at the papers, filled with more pictures than words. "Storyboards?"

Jax nodded, and the green spikes didn't budge.

"For my vision," he said. "I've been waiting years to do this."

Jax looked up at Julia and gathered the pages up again. She averted her eyes to the field, wondering what was so unique that she couldn't see it. Far off in the distance, they'd almost taken the stage down.

"Correct me if I'm wrong," she said, softening her voice, "but I heard you'd left Electric Fury?"

"You're a fan?"

That would work.

"*Huge.* Love your stuff."

"Favourite song?"

Julia hummed the few bars stuck in her head from hearing it on the radio as often as she had. Jax's suspicious squinting softened into a smile. "Great song. One of the best."

"Want to know a secret?" he whispered, pulling Julia in with a finger. "I wrote that song."

"Really?" Julia leaned in. "I heard Jett Fury wrote all the music."

"That's what he told people, but *I* was the one doing all the heavy lifting."

Julia searched for why Mix might have lied about Jax's involvement in the band, but nothing came forward. She'd said he had an ego big enough to clash with Jett's, but with only a fraction of the talent to back it up.

She glanced at the storyboards again.

Stickman drawings.

Coloured in with crayons.

"People should know about this." She gasped, hoping she hadn't taken too long to think about a response. "The fans should know. Jett must have been so jealous of your talents to lie about such a thing."

"Massively."

"Is that why he fired you?"

"I quit." Jax pushed himself up, groaning like Julia did most mornings when she rolled out of bed. He straightened, and she would have guessed he was also in his forties. "Doesn't matter anymore because I'm right where I belong. It's *my* time to shine now."

"Cool hair." She was running out of things to say. "It's so spiky."

"Thanks." He ran his hands up it. "I do it myself. So, you want a picture or an autograph?"

She didn't want either, but she'd come this far.

"Let's make it a picture." Julia patted her pockets down. "Won't be a moment."

She slipped the spare back door key from under the doormat and ran through the kitchen. With all the tables and chairs gone, there was so much more floor space than she'd ever noticed. Like on the morning the letter from the council arrived, she sensed an opportunity.

"This music video," Julia called, scrolling through her notifications as she walked across the yard. She had a missed call from Jessie. "Is it a simple shoot?"

"Simple enough." Clive was the one to reply as Julia pushed through the gate. The three of them were in the alley. "Need a space big enough for some lights, cameras, backdrops, and somewhere to get ready."

"It's so much *more* than that," Jax said, consulting his papers. "There's nothing *simple* about it."

"But on the technical level, Jax." Clive dismissed the flapping of the papers with a wave of his hand before clicking at Julia. "Why are you asking? Do you have somewhere?"

Julia gave the gate a soft kick, giving Clive a clear view into the kitchen. He hurried straight in, ripping through the beads. He didn't need to go any further than the counter.

"Julia, flower?" He strode out with open arms. "Shall we negotiate?"

"Negotiate what?"

A fourth man joined them in his own cloud of smoke, this one smelling more like cherries than a cigar. Detective Inspector John Christie emerged, his eyes going straight to Julia.

"Sorry about this."

"Sorry about what?" Brian exclaimed. "Why are those officers—"

"Julia South-Brown, I'm arresting you under suspicion of harassment," said Christie before reading off the rest of her rights. "Now, will you come quietly, or do I need to cuff you?"

12

"You've just missed lunch," said the officer as he slammed the peephole shut in her cell door. "We're a little backed up on processing today."

"Take your time."

Julia folded the red blanket into a pillow and placed it on the bench. It wasn't much, but it would be comfortable enough for a nap. Olivia had startled her awake through the baby monitor too often in the night to let this opportunity pass her by. Judging by the glares and smirks of the officers she'd passed on her way through the station, they weren't going to rush.

A knock at the door jolted her awake.

Late afternoon going by the light.

They took her to a bathroom and returned her to the cell for another nap.

Gloopy mincemeat and dry mash came through the door a few hours later. She gave it a sniff, the jars of baby food she fed Olivia more appetising. Still, she cleared the tray, making noises as though it was the most delicious meal she'd ever had the pleasure of enjoying. They'd be watching from the camera in the corner, no doubt, but she hadn't given them the satisfaction of more than a glance in its direction.

If they were waiting for her to crack, they'd have to extend the twenty-four hours they could legally hold her.

The door didn't open again until she stood on the bench.

"You're enjoying this, aren't you?" barked Christie. "What are you doing?"

"How are you supposed to see the beautiful sunset?" She pushed onto her tiptoes, fingers clinging to the ledge. "It's like they put it up here on purpose."

"Get down," a sterner voice than Christie's said, and an officer she didn't recognise dragged her off the bench. "Troublemaker."

"Be gentle." Christie opened the door further and clicked for Julia to leave. "If that mob finds out you've hurt a hair on her head, you might incite another riot."

The officer's grip loosened on Julia a little but not entirely. He led her down the brightly lit corridor. All of the other doors were wide open, the cells empty. At the end of the hall, Julia peeked at the reception area through the mesh glass.

She couldn't see her gran, but Dot was certainly making herself heard.

"I should have confiscated that megaphone long ago," Christie said, pushing into a darkened room at the end of another corridor. "You and your family are menaces to society."

"You say menaces," Julia said, tugging free of the officer once she was in the interview room. "I call it a healthy curiosity. Aren't I allowed a phone call?"

The door slammed behind her.

"Sit."

"Not going to offer me access to a lawyer?"

"Just sit down, Julia," Christie muttered, jabbing a button on the recording device. "Interview started at six minutes past twenty-one-hundred hours. By myself, Detective Inspector John Christie. Would you please sit and state your name?"

"My name is Julia South-Brown," she said, still staring at the chair. "And I'm almost certain this is illegal."

He slapped a plastic bag down on the interview table. "What's illegal is this. Care to explain?"

Julia peered down at her notepad. She *had* left it on the chair arm in the salon, the same chair Mix had fallen into after her little trip. Julia was too impressed by the sneaky stunt to be mad.

"If you love something enough, it'll come back to you."

"Enough games, Julia." Christie opened a paper folder and spread photocopied sheets of her handwritten notes across the table. "This could be considered stalking. You know you could be sent down on a harassment charge for this?"

"You know as well as I do that making notes of observations isn't illegal. Let's go through every line. I can easily provide evidence and witnesses to explain my whereabouts."

"You really are your husband's wife."

"Right now, I'm my gran's granddaughter, actually. It's amazing how much law you learn in a neighbourhood watch group." She rocked back on her heels and glanced under the table, unsurprised by what she saw. "I can see that the tape recorder isn't plugged in. What's this?"

Before Christie could stop her, Julia scooped the rest of the sheets from the folder. She was met with diagrams she wasn't holding long enough to take in.

"This isn't a real arrest, is it?"

"It will be once you've been processed."

"I thought we were friends, Christie."

"What does friendship have to do with this?" He straightened out the sheets and spread them out. "You think the fact that your husband used to work here matters anymore? You're constantly making our jobs difficult. Don't you think it's embarrassing for them when the local café owner beats them to the punch?"

"You know that's never my intention."

"And what's your intention this time? Good press for your café's reopening?"

"I hadn't thought of that, but it wouldn't hurt, would it?"

"Or maybe for your husband's failing private investigator business?" Christie smirked up at her, eyes darting to the chair. "He should never have given me his job so freely. What's his yearly salary these days? I can't imagine the royalties from his book are still flooding in."

"It has nothing to do with money," she said, taking the chair finally, "and everything to do with doing what's right. But it's nice to know that's how you think of your friend."

"Barely see the man since your sprog came along."

Christie gritted his jaw, his eyes darting down. She knew from Barker that the only time Christie ever wanted to talk these days was over a pint at the pub, which never ended at one and always ended in teary rants about his divorce or attempts to convince Barker to be his wingman while he tried to "pull" uninterested women. But that was a conversation for Barker to have.

She followed the DI's eyes to the diagrams on the sheets he'd spread. Thin black lines trailed like circuitry around connecting rectangles. At first, Julia thought she was looking at the innards of a fuse box until she saw the labels such as 'DRUMS' and 'VESTRY'.

"This one is a bird's eye view of the rehearsal set up," he explained, tapping his finger down on the first sheet before doing the same to the second. "T*his* is how it usually looks."

Julia scanned both.

"They look the same."

"Almost." He traced his finger along the wiggly lines. "These wires are different. It's subtle, but they're all in slightly different places. Can you see what they're doing?"

Julia remembered the spiral art craze of the nineties with their magical lines converging around a single blank space labelled 'JETT'.

"Everything has been rerouted to run through *this* section," she said, pointing, almost able to feel the moisture. "Exactly where Jett was. You thought this was an accident."

"Past tense," he whispered. "There's little concrete evidence to suggest otherwise, and unless I find some, they're going to draw up a press release and call it a day. I've interviewed them all countless times, and their stories haven't changed a word. They're all saying they don't know who set the space up, and the festival organisers are claiming to have had nothing to do with it. There's a chance their employees are too scared to come forward."

Julia thought back to when she'd asked the question in the flat.

"I think Tia might have been involved in the set-up," she said after a moment's hesitation. "She seemed pretty set on getting me out of the way when I brought it up. I still don't understand how he was electrocuted. The wires must have been exposed under the wet patch?"

"That's exactly what happened." Christie pushed back into the chair. "But can you believe it, they were all faulty after years of being dragged around on the road. And if you think Tia is behind this set-up, she's also the only one who admitted to noticing the damaged wires. She said it was one of the issues she raised when she first joined the band."

"One of?"

"Jett was working her like a dog," he said. "Motive enough in my eyes, but still no evidence to suggest it was her over the others. She said Jett would just seal over the exposed parts with duct tape to stop any conduction, and they'd get on with their shows. There was glue residue on the wires, which could have been from previous set-ups."

"Or someone ripped the tape off, knowing what they were doing?"

"A theory." He nodded in agreement. "But one that can't be proved. Just like we can't prove how the rug got wet."

"Do you know when the rehearsal space was set up in the church?"

"It's one thing I can confirm." He flipped through his own notepad. "Father David allowed them to use the church after Jett threw a hissy fit about the village hall at seven-forty. He didn't see anything else because he left to go and read to the golden oldies at the nursing home."

"And there are no other witnesses who saw people carrying drums and guitars?"

"None that have come forward."

"The village hall is rather close to the church, and if they went in through the back..." Julia stared off into her memories as something dripped down. "When I was selling popcorn behind my café, someone asked for the time, and my father said it was just after six. It was Georgia's friend, Kieran, and Georgia was there too."

"Okay?"

"Well, if the brief downpour was at six, and you're setting up a rehearsal space an hour and forty minutes later, if the floor was somehow still wet, you'd dry it, right?" she said. "Because even if you were setting it up intending to kill Jett, you're not going to want to risk electrocuting yourself in the process. Nor are you going to want the people around you to know what you're up to."

"It could have been set up by one person."

"It could have," she agreed. "But in twenty minutes? I got to the church at around eight. The place was set up with the rug freshly wet. I'd say you can rule out that shower dampening the rug. Tia and Mix were already there."

"They claim to have got there just before Jett did."

"Something must have triggered the electrocution?"

"Tia and Mix claim it happened when he plugged his guitar into his speaker. According to what forensics are putting together, that could be a coincidence"

"But so many coincidences all at once?" She shook her head. "The rain, the wires, the bad electrics?"

"Church's fuse box didn't do its job, so all their circuits were fried in the process. There is another curious thing." He consulted another note. "The forensics report mentioned traces of glue on the fuse box and on the floor underneath it. There's no way to prove why the glue was there, but I believe someone wanted to stop those fuse switches from flipping immediately. By the time the circuit breaker blew its top, Jett was already dead."

"So, someone who knows about electrics?"

"Someone who *thinks* they do," Christie corrected. "Like I said, gluing the fuses down wouldn't have done much, but maybe they thought it would? I can't think of any other reason. And wouldn't you know it, every suspect has some kind of electrical experience in their background."

"Even Georgia?"

"*Especially* Georgia." Another flip of his notepad. "Raised by her father. He was sent down for bank robbery charges at the end of last year, a few weeks after Georgia's mother died. He wasn't the one holding the sawn-off shotgun. He was the man who cut the lights and security systems. Spent twenty years as a professional electrician before that, so you never know what the girl might have picked up. Clive started out in sound engineering. Mix and Tia will know the set-up better than anyone."

"And Jax."

"Jax wasn't in Peridale." Christie consulted his notes. "Arrived by taxi the morning after. We have statements from the driver that brought him from the train station."

"Then I think you should talk to the driver again. Mix is certain she saw Jax on the day of the festival. I told you as much in my original statement."

"She told us that was a joke to wind up Jett."

"And she told me differently this morning before stealing my pad." Julia shook it out from the evidence bag. "I suppose my potential charges trump those of theft?"

"With a surname like Astley-Smythe, yes."

"There were easier ways to pick my brains, Detective."

"All off the record," he said, pointing a firm finger. "And you haven't told me who you think is behind this."

"If I knew, I would." She tucked her pad away, ready to fill the rest of the pages with all the new details DI Christie had so kindly offered. "If there's nothing else, I assume I'm free to go?"

"You're being let off with a caution," he said, wafting his hand to the door. "And please *do* take caution. Keep ruffling Miss Astley-Smythe's feathers, and there won't be much I can do to help you. That family has people in powerful places, and she's not afraid to use her surname. You really spooked her, you know. She was sure you were a journalist. It took everything to convince her you hadn't paid off Katie to lie about your backstory."

Tucking her notepad away, Julia wondered if she'd been onto something with her notes on Mix. Julia was even more curious to talk to her again than she had been the previous two times, though how she was meant to do that without ruffling Mix's feathers, she didn't know.

When Julia had left the salon, she'd doubted Mix's guilt. Now, ignoring smirks identical to the ones she'd received on the way in, she wasn't so sure as she left the station.

13

"*She's free!*" Dot's voice crackled through the megaphone. "There were more of us, but people have more important things to do than fight for justice."

Julia was glad to see only her gran, Barker, and Olivia were left fighting for justice on the busy tables outside The Plough. From the looks of their plates, they'd enjoyed fish and chips for dinner, and from the stares of the villagers having a late-night pub supper, Dot had spent most of the day advertising Julia's arrest.

"I did try to get you out," Barker said, glaring across the road. "That place isn't what it was."

Dot finally clicked off the megaphone and pulled

AGATHA FROST

Julia into a hug. "You look a fright. Have they been interrogating you this whole time?"

"I had a nice nap, actually," she said, pulling away from the hug and going straight to the pram, "and I got some good information."

"Then it's back to mine for a debriefing. We'll get it all written down while it's fresh. You're not the only one who's had a busy day. Your father is telling everyone that you agreed to have a music video filmed in your café. I said you would never agree to—"

"I did." Julia pulled Olivia out of her pram. She was glad to see Barker already opening his car doors. "I'll tell you all about it tomorrow, but right now, all I want to do is go home."

Barker drove Julia home and didn't ask any questions until Olivia was tucked in and Julia was out of the shower. At the table in the back garden, lit by the glow of the kitchen light, she told him everything that had happened. He sighed, rubbed at his stubble, and between rounds of heavy yawning, said he felt responsible.

"Lesson learned. I won't be so careless with where I leave my brain." She patted the notepad. "You should get to bed."

"You must be tired too."

"I wasn't joking about the nap." She stretched out and leaned into the wrought iron chair. "I think we need a new mattress. I feel suspiciously well rested for having slept on a police cell bench."

Julia stayed in the garden, going over her notes and making enough to almost finish the current iteration of her notebook. The bee was buzzing in her bonnet, and it wouldn't leave until she could make sense of what was happening.

By the first creamy hints of the approaching dawn, Julia went into the cottage and wondered if she should crawl into bed, but her nap really had done wonders. She made a coffee instead. Sipping it alone in the toy-filled sitting room in the quiet calm of the early hours, she started a list of the suspects and potential motives.

Mix – Revenge against Jett's treatment.

Jax – Way back into the band.

She realised she was writing them in order of likelihood and assessed Mix's name again. After her day at the station, she was staying at the top of the list.

Georgia – Obsession gone too far.

Clive.

Tapping her pen on the chair arm, she realised Clive might be the only one who'd had something to lose from Jett's death. As much as she didn't trust him, given what she'd seen so far, he'd seemed ready to bend over backwards to provide Jett with what he wanted to further the band, something he didn't seem so confident of now that Jax was in the spotlight. By Mix's own admission, he was decent enough at his job to have had their bookings increase since he'd taken over managing them.

Clive – Ask further questions.

Tia – Worked too hard?

Pen tapping again, she wasn't so sure about Tia's motive either. She'd seen how Jett had treated her, but was that enough to resort to murder? There had to be more to it. She pulled her laptop from underneath the magazines on her coffee table and pushed it open on her knee.

She searched through the websites Barker had printed out, but none were up to date enough to include anything about Tia, not even a surname to search on social media. The Electric Fury accounts made the band look like a Jett Fury solo project. Two festival reviews mentioned that she was new to the band that year and she found a handful of conversations referencing her on message boards. Two people admitted that she was a better drummer than Jax, but the rest were too steeped in nostalgia to accept yet another line-up change. She wondered how they'd react when they found out Jax was back in a new role.

About to close the laptop, she remembered what Mix had said about Jett's first stab at the music industry. What had she said his name was? Jamie … something? If she'd had her notepad, she'd have noted it. Clicking on the 'Video' tab, she typed in 'ELECTRIC FURY MUSIC VIDEO' to no results, only more live performances.

'JETT FURY MUSIC VIDEO'

No results, only live performances.

'JAMIE JETT FURY MUSIC VIDEO'

No results.

She let out a frustrated sigh before finishing the coffee, now cold. It had been something short. A letter of the alphabet?

'JAMIE A MUSIC VIDEO'

No results.

'JAMIE B MUSIC VIDEO'

No results.

'JAMIE C MUSIC VIDEO'

One result.

If it hadn't been for the tattoo under his much more toned belly button, Julia wouldn't have thought the young man barely out of his teens was the same man she'd first seen leaning against the tour bus. Blond curtains framed impossibly blue puppy dog eyes fixed down the camera lens. The video cut from close-ups of his shiny face to wide shots of him dancing like a Backstreet Boy in a well-lit tunnel. She turned the volume up, and like with the spiral art design of the rehearsal space set-up, syrupy nasal vocals reminded her once again of the nineties:

Baby
I need you here
Why'd you have to leave me?
You disappeared
Baby
How you broke my heart.
Can't I stop thinking of you?
Really tears me apart

"A far cry from Electric Fury," she said to Mowgli, whose head had popped up after a key change. "No wonder he didn't trust the record—"

Julia slapped the laptop shut after a bang at the door. Daylight was bleeding through the curtains. A glance at the clock on the mantelpiece let her know it was almost six in the morning.

Slightly too early for her gran.

The letter box rattled.

Far too early for the post.

Putting her pad in the lamp's glow on the side table, she stood up, and Mowgli scurried from where he'd been curled. Julia pulled back the curtains and saw a black hoodie and a backpack.

"Jessie?"

Dropping the curtain, she joined Mowgli in skidding into the hallway. The cat shot through the open bedroom door and bounced off Barker, producing a groan.

"Barker!" Julia called after him. "It's—"

Julia yanked open the door and saw blue.

"Georgia?" Julia stared at the pale face of the teenager. Her eyes were fixed on her black boots. "What are you doing here?"

"*He* said you were looking for me," she muttered, shrinking even smaller as she stepped to the side to show Kieran at the bottom of the path. "He said you could help."

"Who is it?" Barker's hand slipped around Julia's shoulder as he appeared behind her. "*Georgia*?"

"This was a bad idea."

Georgia marched back to the gate, but Kieran turned her back around and sent her up the path. She reached into the backpack, and the rolled-up wad of cash bounced off the doorstep and into the grass.

"Sorry," she mumbled, shrugging.

"Sorry?" Barker laughed. "I'm calling the—"

"There's a more pressing matter to discuss," Julia said, louder, picking up the money. She hadn't had a chance to count it, but if Georgia had pilfered any, she'd left a lot. "You're filthy and shivering. Have you been sleeping rough?"

Georgia shrugged.

"Have you been eating?"

"Sort of." Another shrug. "Well, you've got your money back now, so whatever."

"Barker, make breakfast." Julia opened the door wider. "Full English, and don't miss the trimmings. Kieran? You're joining us."

While Barker cooked in the kitchen, Georgia made use of the bathroom.

"Nice house," Kieran said, taking in the pictures at the mantelpiece. "She turned up at the B&B when I was checking out. I thought she might. She loves to leave things till the last second."

"Did she say where she's been?"

"In that big forest behind the church." Kieran turned without expression, a far cry from the happy-go-lucky boy she'd first met at the festival. "Said she was too devastated after what happened to Jett to see anyone. I'm sorry for bringing her here, but that nice lady who runs the B&B told us where to find you, and you came looking for her, so…"

"I appreciate you coming," she said, offering him a smile. "Have a seat. Breakfast shouldn't be long."

Once she was out of the shower, Georgia refused a change of Jessie's old clothes from a bag Julia had meant to take to the charity shop for months. They ate on their knees in the sitting room, and Georgia picked at her food like someone who wasn't hungry, finishing last. Barker cleared away their plates, leaving the two of them and Mowgli, now on his back in the bright morning sun.

"So, Georgia," Julia started. "You must be a big fan of Electric Fury's music."

Georgia tickled Mowgli's belly. "Not really."

"Then why the stalking?"

"I'm not a stalker."

"If you're not a stalker, what are you?"

"His daughter." She clenched her jaw. "Jett Fury is my dad."

Georgia's delivery should have made it sound like a bombshell, and it might have shocked Julia more if she hadn't heard the truth about Georgia's father during her arrest.

"I never knew Jett had children."

"It was a secret," she said as Mowgli flipped over and hissed at her too rough tickling. "My mum told me before she died. Told me not to go looking for him."

"You've been doing a lot of that."

"He'll understand when I tell him."

Julia hugged her coffee, feeling way out of her depth.

"Georgia, Jett is dead. You must know that."

"Nope." Smiling, she shook her head with clenched eyes. "You don't know him. This is all a stunt. He'll be back at the concert on Saturday. You'll see."

"There isn't a concert on Saturday."

"Yes, there is." Georgia sprang to her feet. "Nobody ever believes me about anything."

"Are you surprised, given your behaviour? Do you have any proof that Jett was your father?"

"Is." Her nostrils flared. "Jett. Isn't. Dead."

"Have you seen him?"

"No."

"Have you heard from him?"

"No."

"Do you have any proof to suggest that he wasn't electrocuted last Friday?"

She shook her head.

"I saw his body with my own two eyes," Julia said as softly as she could. "I know it can be hard to come to terms with the truth sometimes, but you must understand that wanting Jett to be alive isn't the same thing."

"You wouldn't understand."

"Then help me." She ducked to meet Georgia's evasive eyes. "Let's just consider for a moment someone wanted to hurt Jett. If you knew him so well, and you've seen so much, who do you think could be behind something like this?"

"You mean like *her*?" Georgia's voice was filled with venom, and before Julia had time to guess, she said, "You know she was cheating on him? With that idiot?"

"Mix?"

Georgia nodded.

And the idiot?

"Mix was cheating on Jett with Jax?"

Another nod. This time, she produced her phone. Instead of showing Julia something, she tapped her thumbs and Julia's phone pinged where she'd left it in her dressing gown pocket after her shower.

"You had Air turned on, so I sent you proof," she explained. "She thinks Jett doesn't know. He knows everything. He's not stupid. And he's not dead. I know it. My dad wouldn't just leave me like this."

Julia remembered Jett's anger when he'd chased her out of the flat. She could only imagine how tired of seeing her at every stop on tour he had been.

"The day of the festival, you broke into the flat above the post office."

"I just wanted to see him," she said quickly. "To talk to him. To make him understand. He wouldn't listen. If I could just say the *right* thing, he'd get it. He'd want me."

"I know about your real father. The electrician? In prison?"

Georgia's pale blue eyes snapped to Julia. Julia was sure the young girl was about to launch on her. In a flash, Georgia snatched up her things and ran. Julia hurried into the hallway, but Georgia was already sprinting into the fields by the time she reached the door.

"She does this all the time," Kieran said apologetically. "I'm not running after her anymore."

"I'm going to take him to the station," Barker said, clapping him on the shoulder. "First train is in ten minutes. I just need to throw some clothes on."

"I'm already dressed." Julia scooped up her keys.

On the way to the station, Kieran took in Peridale like it was the most beautiful place he'd ever seen. When he ran out of comments for the lampposts and floral displays, the conversation quickly turned back to Georgia.

"She's always asking for favours," he said, his sour

mood returning. "Always coming up with some mad plan to do something."

"Does she come up with a lot of things?"

"Like stories, you mean?" Kieran asked. "She told me this morning that Jett was her dad, and she's been keeping it secret since her mum died. Her mum had a screw loose. She was never really around until she was dying, and then she started filling Georgia's head with nonsense about how her dad wasn't her dad. He was the one who raised her, you know. Her mum was always off doing something. It proper messed Georgia up. I told Georgia this was her last chance, and she promised she wouldn't do anything weird, but here we are. I used to think we were friends."

Julia pulled into the station car park, filled with the few commuters who travelled out of the village for work.

"Maybe one day you'll both look back on this and laugh."

"Nah." Kieran climbed out of the car. "Even after everything, I'm glad I came. It made me realise that she was dragging me along because she needed someone to feed into her delusions. She's used up her last chance with me. Thanks for the lift."

He closed the door and slung the backpack over his shoulder. Julia drove the car to keep up with him and reached across to roll down her window.

"She's denying that Jett is dead," she called. "At the B&B, you said she'd never have killed him. What do you think now?"

"With all the lies she's told me over the years, I wouldn't put anything past her." He pulled a train ticket from his bag. "If you're unlucky enough to see her again, tell her to leave me alone."

As Julia watched Kieran climb aboard, she hoped he was returning home to something calmer. She drove back into the village, which had seemed to be a picturesque postcard through Kieran's eyes. Julia felt the same most days too, but as was the case around Peridale, it was never long until something disrupted the peace.

"Julia!" Her father waved her down from outside the café as she turned into the centre on her way to her lane. "Barker said you'd be coming back this way. You alright to let us in?"

Clive and Jax were waiting behind him, along with four others dressed in dark clothes with a mountain of filming equipment around them. Julia hadn't given the music video a second thought since her arrest.

She remembered why she'd offered her café in the

first place. Better to keep them somewhere she could keep an eye on them. After her arrest, she had nothing but questions for the band. Summoning the remaining energy of the last sip of coffee as the sleepless night started to claw at the edges of her eyes, she climbed out.

"I negotiated the entire deal for you," he said, opening her car door for him. "That's another five hundred for the kitty. Should replace what that girl stole."

Brian was already giddy – hopefully not from champagne so early. He seemed deflated when Julia, barely able to suppress her yawn, didn't immediately join in his excitement.

"The popcorn money came back," she said, climbing out. "Is this money upfront?"

"They're good for it, don't worry," Brian whispered, looping arms as they walked towards the café. "Relax, it's all taken care of."

"That doesn't land like you think it does."

"What do you mean by—"

"Can we get unlocked so we can get started?" Clive called through cupped hands. "Time is money, people. Time is money!"

Julia squeezed through the restless crew. There was a relieved rumble when she pulled out the café's keys. Ignoring the woman holding a large light with her foot already on the doorstep, Clive barged in, and Jax slipped in behind him.

"Lighting, I want the rig up now," Clive's voice echoed behind the blind. "Make-up and hair, kitchen. Cameras, your positions are already blocked out."

Julia followed behind the crew, surprised to see they'd painted one of the walls white. At first, she was relieved to see at least one less spray-painted wall, but they'd done just as sloppy a job as the wannabe graffiti artists.

"Julia?" Clive clicked at her, motioning behind the counter. "Whoever that is, get them out. We can't get any further behind schedule than we already are."

While Clive busied himself positioning a high-backed antique leather chair against the white wall, Julia weaved through the women setting up the cameras. The make-up and hair duo were staring down at something.

"Are they alright?" one of the make-up guys said. "I'm not being paid enough for this."

"Have you even been paid yet?" said the other.

"No."

"Me neither. Do you think they're dead?"

Julia's heart skipped a beat when she saw what they were looking at. Someone in a sleeping bag, their head propped up by a bag, a black hood low over their face. Julia also wondered if they were dead until she heard the gentle snoring. A pair of yellow tags jutted from the Doc Martens next to the bag.

"How did you get in here?" Julia whispered, shaking the feet poking out at the bottom of the sleeping bag. "Georgia, wake up."

The snoring turned to a snort.

But there was no blue hair to be seen as the intruder dragged back their hood – only long dark brown hair framing a freckled and tanned face. Brown eyes blinked up at Julia as they squinted at the light.

Julia tried to talk.

Tried to move.

Tried to do anything.

She was only able to stare.

"Hello, Mum," said Jessie as she pulled out orange earbuds. "I'd say 'surprise', but what was it you said on the phone? 'Everything's fine and there's no need to worry.'"

14

*J*essie rubbed the sleep from her eyes before springing out of the sleeping bag and straight for her shoes. Lacing them up with quick fingers, she tossed her sun-warmed brunette hair over her shoulder.

Julia was in her armchair. Or behind the wheel of her car, drifting between lanes on her way back from the station. Was she in a ditch, about to see a blinding light to leading to the other side?

Anything made more sense.

"Jessie...how...I don't understand."

"I don't know if you've heard, but there are these things called planes. They fly way up above us and carry people around. Tokyo to Taiwan, Taiwan to

Düsseldorf, Düsseldorf to Frankfurt, Frankfurt to London, and then a bus and a train. Did the last bit on foot."

How Julia had missed her daughter's quick wit.

Julia grabbed Jessie into a hug.

The tightest she'd ever given.

"On *foot*?"

"Not in a Frodo walking across Middle-Earth way. Just ten minutes from the station." Julia held tighter. "Mum?"

"Mhmm?"

She'd missed how Jessie smelled.

"I love you *so* much."

She hadn't even known she'd had a scent, but there it was.

"I love you too, Jessie."

"No, really, I love you." She wheezed. "But I think you're about to snap my spine like a baked baguette."

Julia was almost wrapping her arms back around herself, so she let go. She cupped Jessie's cheeks in her palms and couldn't stop scanning. Jessie's ears were filled with more piercings than she'd left with, her cheekbones more defined, freckles more pronounced. Nineteen when she'd left, twenty standing before her now. How could her daughter look so different so quickly? The video calls hadn't done the changes justice.

"You're *real*."

"Yes, Geppetto, I am," Jessie muttered through mushed lips. "Any chance you might be tripping from the spray paint fumes?"

"No, but you're *actually* here." Julia hugged her again, resisting the urge to hold tight. "Christmas..."

"Hope I haven't messed up your 'Welcome Home' party plans." Jessie forced her way out of the hug this time. "You already knew what cake you were going to make, didn't you?"

A globe with candles on every location Jessie and Alfie had visited.

"No."

"Ah, you're only good at lying through the phone, I see." She looked around the cafe and whispered, "Seriously, what in Banksy's name is going on here? If this is your idea of redecorating, I need to see the mood board because I'm not feeling it."

"It's *my* idea of a set," Clive called, clicking his fingers at them as Jax tried to get past to go into hair and makeup. "Now, if you don't mind, please clear off. Things to do. Busy, busy, busy."

"Listen, mate." Jessie slung the backpack over her shoulder and left Julia's side. "I don't know who you are or what you're doing here, but there's only one name above that door. Nobody has earned the right to tell my mum to get out of *her* café. But I'll give you the benefit of the doubt because it's early, and we're all a little cranky before that first coffee."

"Who the hell are you?"

"I'm Jessie. Who the hell are... Oh, and of course, Dot is on her way with tea. And here I thought *everything* had changed around here."

Beyond Clive's stunned expression, Dot rattled around the green with her tea trolley.

"Haven't missed anything, have I?" Dot called, backing the trolley into the café with a clatter over the step. "Thought I'd bring some tea and biscuits before you started shooting..."

Dot abandoned the tea trolley by the door and barged past Clive like a rugby player on their way to score a try.

"Julia, it's Jessie!" Dot held Jessie at arm's length before yanking her in. "Have you been eating? You're skin and bones. Why are you home so early? Have you been wearing sunscreen? And where's Alfie? Oh, Jessie, you're back!"

"That's how I thought I'd react," Julia said, trying to shake away her shock. "You're really here. Let's go somewhere else, and you can explain what's happening."

"My cottage is closest." Dot scooped her arm around Jessie and dragged her around the counter. "I hope you've taken lots of pictures."

Dot led Jessie out of the café, leaving Julia to pick up a second, smaller backpack. She thought about leaving it under the counter, but Jessie was right. Wherever *here* currently was, it wasn't Julia's Café. Not wanting to waste another moment listening to Clive and Jax squabbling over the order of shots, she caught the door before it shut behind them.

"Have you seen Mix?" Tia called from the bench under the café window in a tightly fastened dressing gown. "She's not answering her phone."

"Not since yesterday afternoon."

"She's not answering the door either."

"I can keep an eye out for her?"

Clenching her arms, Tia looked around the green. She offered Julia half a smile and a nod, returning to her phone. Julia stepped back into the road and peered up at curtains fluttering through the wide-open window of Jessie's flat. Given everything she'd seen from Mix so far, she was probably sitting with her feet on a footstool, enjoying everyone running around after her.

Julia hurried across the green, past the hammering and drilling continuing behind the scaffolding at Richie's, and through her gran's waiting open door. She let the bag slide down in the hallway and found Jessie in the middle of the sofa. Percy and Dot were on either side of her, taking turns asking questions while Lady and Bruce vied for attention at Jessie's feet. Percy glanced over the back of the sofa, waving Julia in.

"Why don't we give them some space, Dorothy?" Percy said, shooing the dogs out. "These two have got a lot to catch up on."

"We'll be in the dining room." Dot pushed a plate of chocolate-covered biscuits closer. "When you're done, you can come in and tell us about what happened yesterday at the police station, Julia."

When they were alone, Julia picked up one of the hastily made cups of tea and took a sip, glad of the excess sugar.

"I've missed you so much."

"I've missed you too, Mum." Jessie stood up and twisted her back. She walked over to the window and pulled back the curtain. "You'd think after everything, I'd be used to sleeping anywhere, but floors never get any easier."

"You could have come home to the cottage. I was up all night."

"I know, I can tell." Jessie winked over her shoulder. "My train arrived in the early hours, and I wanted a few hours' kip before everyone freaked out about me being here. Only, I went into my flat to find some woman asleep in my bed. Was that Georgia?"

"Did she have blue hair?"

"Blonde."

"That was Mix."

"And these people are?" Jessie moved over to the window and opened the curtain. "I didn't think so much would have changed so soon."

"It's been a strange week. There's a lot to explain."

"Yes, there is." Jessie turned and folded her arms, a brow arching. "Like, what you were doing at the police station?"

"Ah, I was hoping you'd missed that one."

Jessie picked up a biscuit and sunk back into the sofa. "Arrested, Mum? At your age?"

"There was a *mix-up*, and I was released without charge. It was much ado about nothing, honestly."

"And the café?" Jessie glanced at the window again and sighed. "I've never seen it in such a state. What are they doing? A photoshoot?"

"Music video." Julia took her daughter's hand in hers. "The number of times I've wanted to reach through the phone. I'm so happy to see you, really, but why—"

"I just wanted to come home, Mum." Jessie nudged her with her shoulder. "Can't it be that simple? I'm home in time for your birthday, too. There's plenty of time for explaining and pictures and every piercing story before then, but first, I need to ask you something very important."

"Anything."

"Where's the baby?" Jessie checked under the scatter cushion. "Because I easily owe her, like, a thousand cuddles."

15

*O*livia didn't want a thousand cuddles.

She didn't even want one.

Jessie rocked her for a respectable amount of time, but the more she tried, the more Olivia revealed her tonsils. Jessie passed her sister back to Barker. "Nine months is almost an eternity for her. I know what babies are like. She'll get used to me."

As calm as he'd become around Jessie, Barker had reacted to her sudden return with the same shock and confusion underlying his excitement as Julia had experienced. When Jessie snuck off to wash the flight away, Barker had all the same questions Julia hadn't been able to get the answers to.

"She'll tell us in her own time."

"Julia, are you coming to fill us in?"

Julia obliged her gran, rewinding back to talking with Mix at the salon, through her arrest and the diagrams, to Georgia's reappearance. Dot scribbled it all down on the chalkboard, where the notes from Barker's office had been edited down in Dot's mind-mapping style.

"At least you finally got your money back," Dot said. "Is there any way to get a DNA test done to check if Jett is her father? I still think she's bonkers, but it would be worth proving. I know he's dead, but he's not buried yet. Julia, did Georgia leave any DNA at yours?"

"Just a stained towel," said Barker. "Two, actually. And let's not even go into the ethics of what you just said. Georgia hasn't consented to a test, and Jett is dead."

"Exactly! What does he care?"

Dot added 'DNA TEST' to her ideas section regardless. She added '(DELUSIONAL)' next to it, which Julia thought was the likelier explanation.

"Jax sounds like a more braindead version of Jett," Dot announced as she dusted her hands, taking in her notes. "My money's still on Mix."

"Not illegally gambling again, are you, Dot?" Jessie pushed open the door while towelling her hair. "And things continue to get stranger. Where did your dining room go? Is that a drone?"

"We don't have a drone," Julia said with a laugh, glancing at her gran. "We don't have a drone, do we?"

"It was in the sale!" Dot tugged a box from among the baskets of walkie-talkies and tactical equipment. "You never know when you'll need an aerial view of something."

"And it has good pixels," said Percy. "Or something."

"Just stay away from airports and army bases." Barker glanced at the box over Dot's shoulder. "And don't let Christie see it. The last thing we need is for him to put us on a watchlist."

"We *are* the watch." Dot shook the box. "And now we have the skies covered."

"You've all lost your minds. Drones and a murder investigation chalkboard? What happened to litter picking and food drives?"

"We do those too." Percy patted the pile of cardboard boxes marked 'FOOD BANK'. "We have *varied* charitable interests." He yanked on the wire that pulled the red curtains across the board. "And just like magic, it's a normal dining room."

That trick might have worked when they'd first chosen Dot and Percy's dining room as the hub for the neighbourhood watch, but Julia was seeing it through Jessie's eyes now. It had taken over almost every inch.

Even the family photos had made way for village maps and timetables.

Jessie pulled on the wire and the red drapes whizzed back. "There was a copy of the paper lying around, so I caught up in the bath. From how much you've written about her that, it seems like all eyes are on Mix?"

"Ah, I put that there especially," Dot said, pulling the plastic wrapper off the drone Julia still couldn't believe her gran had bought. "A fresh pair of eyes would do us all good."

"She's just got home. Let her rest a little."

Jessie stayed at the board, taking in the notes.

"It *obviously* can't have been Mix." Jessie faced them for her assessment. "Not unless she was hoping to kill herself in the process of frying Jett. She was right there."

"The wires were concentrated around Jett." Julia consulted her notepad and ripped out the page she'd drawn from memory as well as she could. "All faulty or worn in some way, under the rug without their usual duct tape to protect them."

Jessie flicked through another copy of *The Peridale Post* and flipped to the centre spread timeline Johnny had put together from submitted pictures. "One, two, three pictures of her, all in the two hours leading up to rehearsal."

"Funny dress," Dot pointed out. "I like an outfit as much as the next person, but safety pins?"

"Exactly my point. And unless she wanted to fry herself in the process, she wouldn't have been right there next to him in a dress made of *metal*."

Julia opened her mouth to say something, unable to believe she'd missed such a detail. She'd heard the jangling safety pins with her own ears.

"Fresh eyes." Dot smiled ear to ear, patting Jessie on the shoulder. "Who do you think did it?"

Jessie looked back at the board.

"The stalker seems the most unhinged. If Jett is her dad, then maybe she wanted to get revenge. She's gone out of her way to get his attention and it hasn't worked."

"She's the one who doesn't seem to think Jett is even dead, and I don't think he's really her father," Julia said. "The moment I brought up her real father, she ran off. It was like I'd dared question the lie."

"Maybe it is a lie," Jessie said. "Might not be hers, though. This friend of Georgia's said her mum was always messing with her head. Could have been one final twist on her deathbed?"

"Well, the bonkers girl has a habit of vanishing and reappearing. Considering her most recent reappearance, I'd give it another ten to fifteen business days before we see her again." Dot gave the string a firm tug, covering the board. "Can never be too careful. I swear I saw Ethel White hiding in our bushes the other day, trying to steal our ideas."

"I really do think Peridale's Eyes are as good as done, my love," said Percy. "It's not like we've seen them around lately."

"Then the village will be all the better for it! We only need *one* neighbourhood watch group, after all. They were never up to the job, and we're far superior. We don't need their constant competition."

"All a little dictator-ish," whispered Jessie.

"I say we go and talk to Mix and get the truth from her once and for all. All that girl needs is a straight talking-to."

"When has that ever worked?" Barker laughed. "She already has a relationship with Julia, even if she did hand the notepad over to the police. Julia could offer an apology, and if it's anything like the other times, she'll spill her guts all over again."

"No offence, Julia," Dot said, already walking out, "But you haven't got a straightforward answer from her about anything yet. Miss Astley-Smythe seems to be the queen of contradictions, and given the show she's been putting on, wearing a metal dress is *exactly* the stunt she'd pull to secure her innocence."

∼

With Percy offering to watch Olivia, the three of them followed Dot as she marched across the village green. Even before they reached the flat, it was clear they weren't the only ones looking for Mix.

"Are you surprised she won't come out?" Tia cried at Clive as he banged on the door. "This is humiliating. You can't force us."

"You signed the contract." Jax kicked away from the wall and pointed at Tia. "You're not going to ruin this for me."

"Ruin this for *you*?"

"Just do as you're told."

Tia stormed down the alley, and ran behind the café. Julia noticed the tour bus wasn't where it had been parked all week.

"Don't go too far," Clive called, shaking back his sleeve to look at his watch. "We're finishing this video *today*. Mix, open up!"

Leaving Clive to keep banging, Julia followed Tia. She hadn't gone far. Leaning against the wooden fence where Julia had looked out after so many busy days, Tia's shoulders were hunched like Clive's had been when he'd been whispering with Jax. But Tia wasn't making plans. She was alone and quietly sobbing, trying to keep the tears in. Julia's foot crunched a beer can that had evaded Dot's litter patrol, and Tia's head whipped around.

"Has she come out?"

"Not yet," Julia said over the sound of Clive's continued door banging. "I'd ask if you'd had a rough day at work, but the morning has just started."

Tia stared at Julia with the same distrusting gaze she had in the flat, but it didn't linger. Clutching the dressing gown tighter, she looked worried.

"What do you want?" Tia asked, brushing away her tears. "I don't have to talk to you about anything. You're not the police."

So, the police had been talking to her.

Had Christie followed up on Julia's suggestion that Tia might have set up the rehearsal space? Julia considered the best way to approach asking, not wanting to give Tia room to wriggle out. She opted for daring.

"I know it was you who set up the rehearsal space."

"How did you—"

No denial.

"Because Jett was treating you like a roadie," she said, moving in closer and offering a tissue from the packet she always kept on her. Tia plucked one out and wiped away her ruined eyeliner. "You're too good a drummer to be carrying their bags."

"Paying my dues. I thought he was treating me like that because I was deaf, but Mix said he was the same with her when she first joined, and before he was fired, Jax was still carrying the bags. How did you know it was me?"

"Given how quickly it was set up after the change, I assumed it would have to be someone in the band. But before that, your timing of telling Mix about who my husband was sent up a little red flag."

Tia stared out at the field for a silent moment, with only Clive's letterbox rattling and Jax's demands of the make-up artists filling the quiet country air. In the distance, mist rolled towards the village. The heatwave was well and truly over.

"Yeah, I did set it up," she said. "I always did. Mix usually helped, but she said she..."

"Said she what?"

"Needed to go and get help with something," Tia whispered. "I don't know what, so don't ask. I had to move everything across on my own. I did it *exactly* as I always did. I didn't even know about the rug being wet until the police told me after Jett died."

"Because he had his back to you when he was complaining about it."

Tia nodded.

"I used to try and follow along until I realised they were only ever spitting venom at each other," Tia said. "Too much like my parents. One advantage of not being able to hear is I don't have to put up with it. I just choose not to look at their lips."

No wonder she'd been on her phone when Julia had walked into the church. She imagined every rehearsal started with some back-and-forth bickering between the couple.

"You were there when I followed Jett in."

"I walked around the graveyard to clear my head for the show. It was going to be the biggest crowd I'd played to."

"For how long?"

"Ten minutes?"

"How long did it take you to set up the space?"

"Ten minutes."

No hesitation.

Lined up with what Christie had said about the twenty-minute gap.

"Ten minutes seems quick?"

"I told you, I've been doing it all season. It's not that difficult once you know how."

"Why didn't you tell the police?"

"Because I thought they'd try and blame me. I put tape over the damaged wires like Jett showed me, then left. The rug *wasn't* wet. Mix was already there when I returned after my walk, and Jett came in a few minutes later."

"Ten minutes seems long enough for someone to

move some wires around, rip up some tape, and spill some water."

"Do you really think it was murder?"

The sign for 'murder' was a hand jutting down in a stabbing motion.

"Mum?" Jessie called. "You might want to see this."

Leaving Tia at the fence, Julia returned to the alley. The door was open, but the chain had been pulled across on the inside.

"Come in, Percy." Dot spoke into a walkie-talkie pulled from the back of her skirt. "Can I get a location check from the bedroom window? I need to know if you can see Mix in the flat above the post office. *Over*."

Julia looked at the cottage as the binoculars appeared.

"Curtains are open, the bedroom door is open," his voice came through in stuttered crackles. "Unless she's in the bathroom, the flat seems empty to me. Over."

"But it's latched," Julia mumbled, stepping back to look at the open window. "Maybe she went out the front window?"

"It's way easier round the back."

Jessie nodded for Julia to follow her to the bottom of the alley. Standing where the tour bus had been, she pointed to the bedroom window, open like the front. Even without Jessie tracing the path for her, Julia could see how anyone tall enough could have stepped from the window to the wall and down onto the post office's bins.

"I didn't tell you every time I lost my keys," said Jessie. "Easy way in *and* out."

Jessie launched herself at the wall, much like Georgia had done with the turnstile. She hurried, low like a cat, before pulling herself through the open window. Seconds later, she was at the front door.

"Empty," Jessie said. "I think there's blood on the sofa."

"It's red wine." Julia followed Jessie back up the stairs. "What time did you say you came in and saw her?"

"About half past four this morning."

She sniffed the stain, and it was still only wine.

"Clive, when did you see her last?"

"Last night, just before midnight," he said. "We were meeting about today's shoot. That's when I called bedtime so everyone could be rested for today. Speaking of which, time is money. Where the heck is she?"

Julia looked around the flat for a note explaining Mix's absence but found nothing. From the looks of the messy bedroom and the uncorked red wine next to a freshly poured glass on the dining table, she'd left in a hurry.

"Tia seems quite upset."

"A silly tiff about wardrobe." He flapped his hands dismissively. "She was kicking up a stink about the clothes Jax wanted for the video, but it's nothing to worry about."

"And has Mix ever gone missing before something important before?"

"Not that I can recall."

"Any chance she could have taken the tour bus?"

"It was only a rental for the festival season, and this was *supposed* to be our last show. There was no room in the budget to keep it sitting there."

"Aren't you worried about where she could be?"

"Much like her late husband, she can't get through a work commitment without a dash of drama." Exhaling heavily, he said, "My star client is dead, and I'm trying to make good of a bad situation. If you don't get that, I can't help you, and unless you can find Mix, you can't help me. Any more than you already have, of course. Now, if you'll excuse me, I have a music video shoot to salvage."

Clive hurried down the stairs, and Julia joined Jessie, who was crouched in the bedroom under the window, next to a plant – the monstera that had caused so much trouble in Julia's early watering day.

"Confession time," Julia said, squatting next to her.

"I killed the one you originally had here and replaced it. I hoped you wouldn't notice."

She swept the leaves to the side. "I hadn't, but I did notice *this*, and I know *I'm* not bleeding."

A thin line of blood ran from the windowsill to a pool the size of a button on the carpet. There wasn't much, but it was fresh enough that the centre was still gleaming against the dried edges.

"Oh, Vivienne," Julia said, looking out at the empty field. "What have you got yourself in the mix of this time?"

16

"Christie's telling everyone not to jump to conclusions." Barker joined Julia on the café's backstep. "Apparently, there are *many* ways that blood could have got there."

Julia couldn't believe her ears. "She either went of her own free will and injured herself on the way, *or* she was taken. It was only yesterday he told me he thought something was going on."

"That was when it didn't directly affect an Astley-Smythe."

"Sneaking out through the back window doesn't strike me as a Mix thing to do. But what do I know? Maybe this was her plan all along."

"We did think she seemed the most likely suspect."

Not anymore.

Julia looked ahead at the end of the foggy field. Like when she'd looked out to see the stage on the morning of the council letter, it seemed something else was being built.

"We can't give up," Julia said, more determined than ever. "We have to figure this out. It's gone too far, and—"

"What now?" Barker huffed as a commotion came from the alley. "Let's hope she's back."

Julia left the yard, but before she could reach the alley, she noticed DI Christie at the open window of Jessie's bedroom.

"You found the blood, and I found the hair." He hurried down the stairs with a shiny, electric blue strand pinched between gloved fingers. He gave it a few tugs, and it hummed like a guitar string. "And there's several. Looks like Georgia has finally given us the evidence we need."

As the hair went into a plastic evidence bag, Julia was sure it wasn't one of Georgia's hairs. Like her first magenta buttercream attempt, the hue was far too saturated compared to the softer, creamier aqua blue she'd been seeing all week. She opened her mouth to say as much to Christie, but would it matter?

"I've been meaning to call," Barker started before

Christie rushed off. "Georgia was at our cottage this morning, and she had a lot to say."

"And I'm hearing about this *now*?"

"She ran off before we had the chance to stop her," said Julia. "I think she's been sleeping rough in Howarth Forest."

"Search the forest," Christie barked at a group of officers. "Find Georgia *now*!"

Later that night, Julia rested her head against Barker's shoulder at the kitchen sink. Through the window on the patio, Jessie was trying her hardest to interest Olivia in her paddling pool toys, but she was too busy splashing.

"Has she mentioned if this is a flying visit?"

"I haven't asked."

"And Alfie? You could always call him to ask."

Julia had considered calling Jessie's once estranged older brother, but he hadn't come up at all since her return. She didn't want to go around her if something had happened.

"It'll come out in her own time."

While Barker got ready for bed, Julia stayed at the window, drying the dinner plates from the stir fry. It really was great to have their family together again.

Still, Barker's comment about the flying visit made her realise she'd avoided asking the question all day because she didn't want to think about Jessie leaving again so soon. Jessie had said she'd wanted to come home, which had to be enough for Julia right now. She wasn't going to let the "why" get in the way of enjoying their time together, however long it did or didn't last.

"You two look like you're having fun," Julia said, scooping Olivia out of the water. "Weather's getting chillier by the hour, and I think it's time to get this one ready for bed."

"I can do it." Jessie tried to take Olivia, but the baby clung to Julia. "I can't say it doesn't sting, but I won't hold it against you."

Julia carried Olivia through to the bathroom and turned on the taps, and Jessie followed, scooping up crumpled black socks from the tiles and opening the washing basket.

"You'd think Dad would be house-trained by now." Staring into the basket, she added, "Whose idea was it to make white the standard colour for towels?"

Julia looked down at towels with only white edges remaining in a mess of blue. She could almost see Georgia ruffling them without caring if she was staining them. She plucked one of the many hairs Georgia had deposited on the towel and held it up to the light like Christie had done in the alley. She couldn't give it a few tugs because it snapped at the slightest pressure, as did two more.

"I was sure then, and I'm even more sure now. Someone planted that hair in the flat."

Julia twisted off the taps and stared at herself in the water's calm surface. Georgia had proven how far she'd go with her questionable behaviour and possible lies. As agile as the teenager was, and however big a bag she could carry, there was no way she could have taken Mix from the flat via a second story window.

"Go on, get out," Jessie ordered, opening the door. "I've got this one. Get your ideas down."

"Oh, it's—"

"I know what I'm doing." Jessie checked the water with her elbow. "Grew up in foster care, remember. I was a live-in babysitter for half of those placements as soon as I was old enough to pick them up. Don't you trust me?"

"You know I do."

"Then let go," Jessie said, directing a pointed look at Julia's fingers clenching the edge of the door. "I know you like to do a lot on your own, but I've got this. Takes a village to raise a kid, and all that."

Julia left Jessie and went to the sitting room. She picked up her notepad, sat in the armchair by the fireplace with the open bathroom door still in view, and flicked to a new page. She headed it with "Georgia" and then started a list:

Obsessive.

Unpredictable.

Liar.

Wagging the pen, Julia stared ahead at the window as the sun set on another day in which she hadn't figured this out.

Short.

Nimble.

Strong.

"You paint a compelling picture." In his pyjamas, Barker propped himself on the armchair. He blocked the view to the bathroom, though from the sounds of it, Olivia was finally enjoying Jessie's company. "Bit of good news. John just called. They've found her."

"Mix?"

"Georgia. Howarth Forest, just like you said."

Wishing she wasn't so disappointed, Julia tried to focus on the fact that Georgia was alive and well. After seeing the hair, she didn't think Georgia was behind this any more than she thought Mix was.

"Can you believe I was trying to think of reasons she didn't do it?"

"John's latest theory is that Mix killed Jett, Georgia knew, and this is her way of getting revenge. He described her using half of those words you've just written down. You said yourself that Georgia seemed to hate Mix for her affair with Jax."

"We still don't know that she was having an affair with him." The pen continued to wag. "I know Georgia's a troublemaker, but she did all those things to get Jett's attention, not to kill him. Why would she be denying that Jett was even dead if she killed him?"

"Maybe she can't face what she's done?"

Jessie left the bathroom with Olivia wrapped up in a fresh towel and went to the nursery. Julia pushed herself out of the chair, but Barker shook his head.

"Jessie's waited nine months, too. Let's give her a chance to get to know her sister without sticking our noses in."

"You're right."

Julia sank back into the chair and returned to the pad. She flicked through the reams of notes from her observations of Mix. It had been easier to believe the socialite-turned-guitarist was behind the death of her husband when she'd been around to show her mood swings.

"What are we missing, Barker?"

"How tired you are. The police have Georgia and will interview her as soon as she has a lawyer present. She's not afraid of talking, so maybe they'll have this whole thing wrapped up with a bow in time for a press conference tomorrow morning."

"I hope so," she said, pushing herself from the armchair, "because if Georgia isn't behind this, someone out there thinks they got away with killing Jett. They didn't even wait a week to strike again, all while trying to frame a teenager in the process."

"Mix could still be alive, and there's still a chance that blood isn't hers. Like I said, we might know everything by morning."

Hoping that would be the case, Julia used up the last of the hot water before crawling into her dressing gown. She wrapped her dark curls in a towel and popped her head around the edge of the quiet nursery. Olivia was asleep in Jessie's arms, bathed in the glow of the golden constellations projecting from the nightlight. Jessie was holding a tatty paperback copy of *The Wonderful Wizard of Oz,* passed down from Dot's childhood. Head bobbing, Jessie snorted herself awake.

"You really do get used to sleeping anywhere when you're on the road," she blurted. "Can I kip on your couch tonight? Dot offered her guest bedroom, but I'm not sure I'm in the mood to hear the chalk scratching."

Once Olivia was peacefully asleep in her cot and Jessie was doing the same under a spare duvet in the darkened sitting room, Julia joined Barker and Mowgli in the bedroom.

"I've been researching these Astley-Smythes," he said, peering over the top of his laptop. "The police, the council, the government, even a couple of judges. They really are everywhere. I'd be thinking I was about to lose my job if I was in John's shoes too. Mix's disappearance is boosting the story in the national press. And your pocket is lighting up."

Julia reached into her dressing gown and pulled out her phone. She hadn't worn her dressing gown since her post-arrest all-nighter. Had she gone about the rest of the day without it? From the station to Jessie's return to Mix's disappearance, she hadn't needed to reach for it once.

A wall of notifications greeted her, the familiar names among them:

Gran – Six missed calls.

Leah Burns: Hey, are you free to talk about my wedding cake this...

Roxy Carter is asking for a life on Candy Splash.

Check out the latest activity on Peridale Chat.

Julia was about to plug it in to charge when an unusual name – for her phone, at least – made her pause.

Image received via Air from Georgia Kingsley.

In the chaos of the day, Julia had forgotten all

about her phone pinging in the other room when Georgia was here. What was it she said she'd sent?

"Why didn't I look at this right away?" she said after tapping the image. "Turns out Georgia and Mix *were* telling the truth about Jax being here before the festival, and Mix did more than see him. She told me she hadn't spoken to him."

Climbing into bed, she showed him an image of Mix and Jax on the sofa in the tour bus, taken from around the edge of the doorframe. Mix was in her metal dress, and Jax in a hoody that he'd pulled up over his head, but the neon green couldn't be ignored any more than their pressed-together foreheads and hand holding.

"They look a little closer than former bandmates."

"Mix gave me the impression that she thought he was a loser."

"You said yourself, she wasn't happy with Jett. Maybe they've been working together this whole time."

If so, there hadn't been much harmony since Jett's death. She'd believed Mix when she'd said Jax's attempts at emulating Jett were going to doom the band – a band which she'd admitted she needed to stop her from grovelling at her parents' feet. And why bring up that she'd seen Jax at all if she'd known what was to come?

"She could have fled right away," she said, sliding under the covers.

"Maybe she anticipated it looking like an accident?"

Closing her eyes, Julia let her thoughts wander, and they returned to something she'd said to DI Christie. If Mix, or any of them, had wanted to kill Jett, there were easier ways to do it, even with limited access.

Why electrocution?

And why at the rehearsal?

17

"Coffee?" Jessie's voice made Julia jump. "What happened to the peppermint and liquorice tea?"

Julia was sure she'd have remembered Jessie was sleeping on the sofa if she'd taken her first sip before making Olivia's breakfast. "Pushed back to the afternoon. You can blame your dad for getting me hooked on this stuff."

"And I'm sure this little one helped."

Julia felt a heady rush as Jessie sat at the breakfast bar in her old pyjamas, saved in the bag that hadn't made its way to the charity shop. For a flash, she was that teenage girl once again who'd staggered from her bedroom for breakfast before they headed down to the café. Olivia's babbling at the sight of her sister kept Julia firmly planted in the here and now. Last night's bonding had done their relationship a world of good.

"Coffee must taste good from how much you're smiling."

"I'm just savouring the moment." Julia poured Jessie a cup, her smile growing. "I'm glad we're all back together."

"All?" Barker muttered on his way from the bedroom to the bathroom. "I feel left out."

Julia and Jessie laughed, and Olivia joined in. Mowgli stalked through the open bedroom door and hopped up onto the counter. As excited as ever to see the cat as he rubbed himself against Jessie's shoulder, Olivia's hands slapped down on her highchair tray, and the porridge jumped to its demise. Mowgli didn't stick around to hear the plastic bowl bouncing against the tiles.

"Ah, it's good to be home." Inhaling, Jessie let out a wide-armed stretch. "So? Who's first on your list for a good ol' interrogation today?"

Before the day swept her away, and with last night's notes still singing the same tune, she followed the music to the village green – literally.

"I've heard better singing from drunks at the pub," said Jessie. "Thank whoever's screaming for my bleeding ears."

Standing on the corner outside her gran's cottage, Julia winced in the direction of her café as Jax's electronic screeching fought against a shaky guitar solo. Like her taste buds knew when one of her bakes wasn't quite right, Julia's ears knew Jax wasn't hitting any of the notes he was aiming for. If this was the demo Mix had been sure would end the band, it wasn't stopping the music video shoot going ahead inside her smoky café.

"Why don't we go and see Dot and Percy?" Jessie called to Olivia as she tilted the pram onto the kerb. "Another day of not showing them my travelling pictures, and I'm sure they'll hunt me down."

"And I have a client meeting," said Barker. "*Potential* client meeting, I should say. I wasn't going to say anything but..."

Julia waited.

"You can't leave it there, Barker."

"I *think* it might be the Astley-Smythes."

"Think?"

"They're being very mysterious," he said quietly, kissing her on the cheek, "and they sounded incredibly posh on the phone. Are you crashing their music video?"

"Would be a waste of an opportunity if I didn't."

The villagers dotted around the green couldn't take their eyes away from the window as a red light flashed in a cloud of swirling smoke. She could just about make out hints of neon green hair catching the light in the thick fog.

"You're doing it *wrong!*" Jax cried over the music. "It's supposed to be side to side."

"What does it matter?"

Cupping her hands to the window, Julia looked inside her café. The chunky camera and professional lighting equipment had gone. Instead, Clive was clenching a phone while he stomped on a switch for a lamp with an exposed red bulb.

"Side to side!"

"This isn't easy."

"It's *my* vision."

"Maybe you're blind!" Clive lowered the phone. "I think we got it. Get ready for the next look."

Clive opened the front door but overlooked Julia as the smoke bled out. After going down the alley, Julia heard the rattling beads as she snuck in through the back. Sitting on the corner stool, Jax dragged a mirror through the scattered make-up. Half were still wrapped in plastic, clearly bought recently.

"It's you," he stated, barely glancing at her. "What do you want?"

Julia wondered if she should pull her phone out and show him the image, but she decided against it. With the right notes, she was sure she could get Jax to sing his part.

"Mix told me the two of you were close," she said, leaning against the counter across from him. "You must be quite worried about her. Have you heard anything?"

Jax hesitated with the red kohl pencil pressed to his waterline.

"I haven't."

He added another layer and moved closer to the mirror. If he was worried about her, he wasn't showing it.

"You're filming the video without her?"

"That's showbiz."

"Well, you've got everything you ever wanted." Julia intentionally paused, but Jax didn't offer any reaction. "Everyone wants to be the frontman, right?"

"I didn't *want* Jett's place." He moved on to his other eye. "I *deserved* it. He never gave me credit for any of my genius. He never appreciated what I had to bring to the table. My ideas were never good enough."

"Didn't you say you wrote all the songs?" she asked, keeping her casual tone. "Sounds like your ideas were good enough."

Jax blinked red streaks down his cheeks.

"Ugh. You've made me mess this up!"

"Call it art and move on." Clive burst through the beads, eyes on his watch. "Can we get this thing rolling? I have somewhere else to be."

"How could you have anywhere else to be? I'm your star client."

"You will be after the showcase, which is what I need to organise if we're going to get you that record deal."

"What happened to 'as good as done'?"

"And it is." Clive patted his pockets before glancing at Julia. She darted her brows towards the no smoking sign, and he returned to his watch. "If *you* deliver the goods on Saturday."

Showcase.

Saturday.

Georgia had said there'd be a concert on Saturday.

One truth among many lies?

"One member dead and one missing." Julia followed Jax into the café as Clive fanned the smoke out through the front door with menus in each hand. "And you're putting on a showcase?"

"He tried to sell it to me as a remembrance show for Jett," said Tia, standing up from a chair in the corner as the smoke cleared. "Surprised you're not pretending it's a show to raise awareness for Mix being missing."

"Hey, not a bad idea," said Clive. "Are you ready to film your part now?"

Julia hadn't seen the outfit that had made Tia feel so uncomfortable, so it was nice to see how confident she seemed as she rose wearing a full leather jacket with matching trousers. While Clive dragged away the antique chair, Tia assembled the drums at lightning speed. She glanced at Julia, but she didn't seem as ready to talk today. Through the clearing smoke, Jax's spikes stuck up from the bench in front of the window.

"What now?" He huffed when Julia sat down. "I'm trying to get in the zone, and you're distracting me."

"Then I'm afraid this will only distract you further." Her phone was already open on the image. "Taken on the festival's first day on the tour bus. Care to explain?"

Jax stared dead-eyed at the image before passing it back.

"No."

"You're quite close."

"We're praying," he said. "What's it to you?"

"Don't suppose this had anything to do with Jett kicking you out of the band?"

Crossing his legs, he closed his eyes and pointed his face at the sun. Julia wasn't going to give up so easily.

"Lying won't help you now," she said, tucking the phone away. "But I'm sure the police will make of this what they will if they don't already have it. I hear they're talking to the person who took the picture as we speak."

"Fine," he said, jaw gritting. "I came in on the day of the festival. Had a meeting, and I didn't want Jett to know I was here. He throws a tantrum every time he sees me ever since he sacked—"

"Ah."

"*Fine.*" He unfolded his legs and forced himself up. "What's your problem? You're not a fan at all, are you?"

Had it taken this long for the penny to drop?

"I'm just trying to get somewhere in life, okay? What's wrong with that?"

"Nothing, if you're not hurting people to get there."

"I didn't kill either of them."

"Will you get back here so we can shoot this thing?" Clive barked.

Jax did as he was told, glaring at Julia all the way to the door. He'd already given her more than she could have hoped for. She'd expected him to deny the picture, but he'd instead admitted to lying about his arrival and quitting the band.

And he seemed to think Mix was dead.

Julia hoped that was an assumption and not a slip of the tongue.

"Brian's daughter." Clive waved her over, still half leaning out the door under the sign with her name on it. "Look, I get it. You like to know what's happening around here. But just today, so we can get this done, can I have some grace?" His hands were clenched. "I need this to work as much as these two do. It isn't the best economy for us freelancers right now. You'll understand. This record deal will change everything for all of us."

"And you're hoping Mix will turn up before your show?"

"I'm afraid I can't wait around to find out." Clive looked up the road as a taxi ground to a halt outside the post office. "Ah, that'll be him."

A man in a navy polo shirt and thick-rimmed glasses, with a noticeable comb-over, climbed from the car. He shook Clive's hand, his smile tight and clearly forced.

"I want half upfront."

"Plenty of time for that. It's great to finally meet you."

"Gef?" Jax laughed from the doorway of the café, shaking his head. "No way! You look like an accountant with three kids."

Gef, the bassist Mix had replaced, pushed up his glasses.

"I *am* an accountant with three kids." He looked Jax up and down. "I see you're still doing the exact same thing."

"My hair was black back then." Jax took his former bandmate into a hug but Gef didn't remove his hands from the pockets of his cargo shorts. "Oh, it's terrific to see you, man. *Ha!* Look at you. Unbelievable."

"Nothing eyeliner and ripped clothes won't fix." Clive clicked at the door and turned back to Julia. "Like I said, if you'll just give us the afternoon, I'll talk to you when we're done. I think I know something that'll help your little investigation."

Clive didn't stick around, but he had agreed to talk to her, and she hadn't needed to ask. Already wondering what he could have, she set off across the green. Shilpa was doing the same from the direction of the post office.

"Dot calls these meetings far too frequently," Shilpa said as they caught each other up. "What's it about this time?"

"Not too sure, but I think I have something to add to the board." Julia looked back at the bench where Jax had confessed to his lies. "And apparently, there's more to come."

18

*W*ith Dot and Percy engrossed in Jessie's travelling pictures in the sitting room, Julia and Shilpa snuck through to the dining room unseen.

"Some people are saying that on the forums," Shilpa said, tapping the theory that Mix had killed Jett and then went on the run under the circled 'CONCLUSION' section. "She's got away with it and is pretending to be missing."

Would anyone do that?

Julia wasn't so sure.

"Is that what you think?"

"Oh, I don't get involved in all that." Shilpa took her usual chair. "There's far too much gossip around here to follow all the stuff online *but* I do like to read it. And people have all sorts of theories. I saw someone this morning suggesting that Gef was coming back to the band to take Mix's spot."

"Didn't you see that man getting out of the taxi just now?"

"That was *Gef*?"

"Accountant with three kids."

"Well, I suppose most people grow up and put away the toys one day." Shilpa picked up the drone, now out of its box. She turned it over in her hands, and a chunk of the plastic cracked. She bent it back, and the thing snapped off entirely before she put it down. "Oops. I'd love to know what went through her head when she bought this. We're never going to use it. Remember when we used to have food and laugh at these meetings? Speaking of which, is it just us now? Feels like our days might be numbered."

"Let's save the group politics," said Julia, stepping back to find a spot to add her newest details. "Another day and another member change, and Electric Fury continues to charge on like nothing is happening."

"Sad we never got one final performance with all three of them if Gef was willing to come back."

"I think the coins lured him back."

"Still, they're never going to believe this on the forum. People are already confused about what's going on. Quite a few think this whole thing is one giant press stunt."

Rolling a fresh stick of chalk between her fingers as she searched for a space to squeeze in her notes, Julia considered her final thoughts before drifting off to sleep the night before.

Why electrocution?

Why the rehearsal?

Before thinking about it, she picked up the duster and wiped the board in broad sweeps. Dot rushed in, gasping as she pulled Julia back as she cleared out the final corner.

"Have you lost your mind?" Dot cried. "I was about to crack it!"

"We need a new approach."

"We *needed* those notes!"

"And if you're right about Mix hiding somewhere, thinking she got away with this, I'm sorry in advance, but I don't think that's what's happening here. I've seen her in an unhappy relationship and grieving. Still, if she wanted to kill Jett, she could have done it any place, any time." Julia split the board in two with a white line. She snapped the chalk and passed half to her gran. "I don't think she's an angel, but I don't think she killed her husband. I don't think any of this is about Jett being a bad husband."

"But it might be about Jett being a bad father,"

Barker said as he marched into the room, phone in his hand. "Police have just confirmed it."

"Georgia *is* Jett's daughter?" Julia asked. "DNA test?"

Barker nodded.

"Ha!" Dot tapped the board with the chalk. "That was one of my ideas."

Julia couldn't engage with her grandmother's need to be correct. She was too busy with the shrinking walls of the dining room.

"Definitely?"

"She's made a lot of wild claims, but she gladly consented to the test. This changes everything."

Julia leaned against the sideboard and tried to blow the walls away with a calming breath. She'd been sure Georgia was swimming in a sea of delusion, but she'd been honest about the showcase and her parentage. Julia looked back to the board she'd just scrubbed clean, uncertain.

"Does it strengthen or weaken her case?" asked Julia.

"For now, the public needs a prime suspect. She's filling that role until they need to charge or release her later today." He let Olivia go to Percy, who was flipping coins in and out of existence with his fingers. "If it was my investigation, she'd be at the top of my list."

"And she was right about this."

Julia showed them all the image of Mix and Jett.

"How long have you had this?" Dot demanded, taking the phone. "S*ee*! Mix did it. I know it. Look at them all cosied up. They're seconds from eating each other's faces. What does Jax have to say for himself?"

"He says they're praying." Julia took the phone back. "Shilpa, do you know if Jax is religious?"

Shilpa searched her mental Electric Fury database.

"All of the original members did a twelve-step Alcoholics Anonymous program not long before Gef left, and that's Christian, isn't it? And speaking of Gef, I don't think Mix is behind this. I think it was Gef."

"Gef?" Dot cackled. "He hasn't even been a suspect!"

"Well, that's what *I* think."

Percy's sleight of hand magic couldn't quell Olivia's tears from the suddenly raised voices. Her wails weren't enough to stop their bickering. Taking her daughter as the walls continued to close, Julia carried on down the hallway and out into the humid afternoon air. Thick clouds circled, and from the slightly metallic hint in the air, she could sense a storm was on its way.

"John has the picture of Mix and Jax from Georgia's phone," Barker said, putting his hand on her shoulder. "The electrician is on the birth certificate, and he referred to Georgia as his daughter in his statements when asked about his life. Georgia confirmed that her mother told her the truth on her deathbed. Georgia isn't the only one linked to the band with criminal convictions. Her mother was a groupie in their early days. Followed them everywhere. She had an assault charge for attacking Jett. Almost scratched his eyes out. Going from Georgia's date of birth, her mother would have been four months pregnant with her."

"Georgia's first rejection from Jett Fury."

Julia's heart raced as fast as the frenetic drumming from the café.

"Given her track record," Barker said, even softer this time, "it was the conclusion I'd have come to in your shoes. You were also right about the hair not being hers. It's not even human hair. It's from a wig."

The drumming stopped, but Julia's mind was already racing to the rhythm in the sudden silence.

"Then it proves someone tried to frame her?"

"They're performers." Barker didn't sound so sure. "It's not out of the realm of possibility for them to have wigs with them. Not that I saw any pictures of them in any kind of wigs in my research, nor were there any in their belongings. And there's plenty of trace evidence of Georgia in the flat, which could be from the break-in."

"Why the rehearsal?" she repeated. "Every suspect had direct access to Jett. Georgia could have killed Jett in the shower. Why go to all this trouble?"

Across the green, Tia charged out of the café while ripping off the leather jacket. Clive ran after her, ducking as she threw her drumsticks at him. In the silence, Julia heard them clatter against the road.

"Take a ten-minute break," Clive cried after her, not that she was looking at him to lipread. "You can't leave."

Scooping up the sticks, Clive offered a genial smile around the green before slamming the café door behind himself. The letterbox rattled, and with Jax back in the chair, the terrible song from earlier once again started from the beginning. Olivia had stopped crying on her own, her attention fixed squarely on the light flashing red through the smoke.

At a glance, it looked like the café was on fire.

"How did your meeting go?"

"Terribly," he said, sighing. "It was one of Astley-Smythe's manservants. They made it quite clear they were only interested in finding Mix to save face for the sake of their reputation. Didn't try to hide the fact her parents saw her as a stain on their lives. Gave me a lot of sympathy for her."

"I'm guessing you didn't get the case?"

"Didn't hide that they didn't think I was up to the job, either, which is a shame because he made it clear there'd be no amount too great to find her. I'm not surprised she ran as hard as she did. Speaking of which, if you hurry, you might be able to catch up with Tia." Barker took Olivia before Julia had to declare her intentions. "I'll see if they've calmed down enough to make heads or tails of what's going on."

After checking the fence behind the café for Tia, Julia spotted her rushing past Jessie's bedroom window. Given the lack of evidence left behind, it seemed the police were already done with their search. Julia crept up to the flat, not wanting to startle Tia, though she still managed to do so.

"Looking for something?"

"My contract," Tia said, throwing cushions from the sofa. "It was here in a binder."

Julia remembered seeing the black binder with the gold lettering when she'd brought Mix the wrapped food. She looked to the table. It was still there, but open and empty.

"I hate it here," she cried, fists clenched at her head. "I just want out."

Julia guided her onto the sofa, avoiding the red wine stain, then she took Tia in her arms as she wept. She didn't try to hold them in silently this time.

"What did I do to deserve this?" Tia said through broken sobs. "I thought this was going to be my big break, and they're trying to take it away."

"You're being kicked out of the band?"

"I wish! Because of the contract I signed with Jett, I'm not allowed to *leave* the band. Five years minimum, and if I do leave, there's a fine. Twenty thousand."

"That can't be legal."

"He trapped me. Now he's dead, and they're using it against me. Drumming is the only thing I've ever loved. I've never heard another person's voice or a song, but I always loved how the music made me *feel*. I first picked up a pair of drumsticks in a music shop. I'd always known I loved the vibrations of the heavy drum songs. That feeling going up my arms and me being the one who was controlling it. It's all I've ever wanted to do since. I just want to drum. That's all. I didn't want any of *this*."

Julia could only offer a comforting arm around the young woman's shoulders. She didn't know what to say to make everything better.

"I should have stayed here last night," she said softly. "But I couldn't deal with another night of not knowing which Mix I would get. When she bought the red wine after the meeting, I went to the B&B."

"The meeting about the video?"

"You mean the meeting where Jax and Clive tried to steamroll Mix and me into wearing their stupid costumes?" Tia leaned forward on her knees and forced her hands into her hair. "You know Jax wanted us kneeling on either side of his chair in bikinis? He's a degrading pig."

"That's disgusting."

"Mix warned me at my audition that this band would destroy me like it destroyed everyone else. I thought she wanted to be the only woman or whatever, but she's the only one who looked out for me in any way. I should have listened."

"How did you get into the band?"

"Jett was scouting at a bar where I was playing solo. I went to twenty-four auditions after finishing university. Bands, labels, you name it. They couldn't look past my disability to see it as the asset it is in this industry. So many drummers lose their hearing from the noise, but nobody else could see that this is what I was *born* to do. They assumed I wouldn't be able to keep up or stay on rhythm. There's so much more to sound than what you *hear*. Not until Jett. He was the only one who gave me a chance. Maybe he thought I'd fall in line easier than Jax, but I didn't care. It was an opportunity, so I signed without even looking at the small print, and now Jax is holding it over me in a way Jett never did. I'm stuck with his 'creative genius' for the next four years and four months."

"For what it's worth, I have it on good authority that you're a far better drummer than Jax," she said, resting a hand on Tia's shoulder. "And I'm no musical expert, but if he drums anything like he sings and plays the guitar, Jett was lucky to replace Jax with you."

"Is he *that* bad?" Tia laughed. "I wondered why Clive was sweating whenever I could see him telling Jax how great the demo sounded. Mix wouldn't talk about it. I don't think she wanted me to freak out, but we are doomed. I need to find those contracts. They were here."

Tia pushed off the sofa and went into the bedroom to continue her search. Julia joined her, just as curious about where they could have gone.

"Maybe the police took them?"

"They said the binder was already empty," she said. "I spoke to them, told them about setting up. Some dog walkers saw me walking around the graveyard and came forward last night. My mum said I was an idiot to get my cheeks pierced, but they said it was the only reason they looked at me. I was lucky they didn't charge me for not telling them sooner."

Tia knocked over a backpack leaning against the drawers. A make-up bag toppled out, and among the eyeliners, mascaras, and lipsticks was a gold coin. Julia picked it up; it was like no money she'd ever seen. Across the top, above a large '5', a simple message.

'One day at a time.'

Exactly what Barker had said to her that first morning back at the café.

"Is this yours?"

Tia glanced at it and shook her head before checking the bathroom. Julia had never seen one, but she was sure it was a sobriety chip. She recalled her conversation with Mix in the salon, specifically how she hadn't wanted to talk about her "all a blur" partying days. With what Shilpa had revealed about the original members' stint in AA, she reconsidered what she'd seen in the picture taken on the tour bus. The same bus on which her father had been guzzling the cheap champagne that Jax apparently thought he was too good for.

"When I asked where Mix was, you said she was going to get help for something," Julia asked after catching Tia's eye. "You said you didn't know what, but I have an idea. Do you know if Mix has ever had issues with drinking?"

"Aside from the present issue?" Tia asked.

"Actually, now that you mention it, she didn't drink when I first got into the band. It's got worse this festival season the more we've been touring."

Maybe not an affair, after all.

Putting the chip back into the bag, Julia left Tia to continue searching for her contracts. She returned to her café, where the shoot was ongoing. Jax's spikes wobbled, his neck twisting as he screamed along to what sounded like a chorus of a song she hadn't heard before.

"What did I ask?" Clive urged, pausing the music. "Just give us the—"

"You haven't paid me yet." She remained firm. "If I remember correctly, my father negotiated for you to film the video here *yesterday*."

"And you know how that turned out."

"Does that change the fact I didn't have access to my café?"

Gef laughed as he applied eyeliner in a hand mirror in the corner. Clive glared at him, but he was all smiles when his eyes finally reached Julia.

"Quite right," Clive said, putting the phone on the counter. "Apologies, flower."

"My name is Julia, flower."

Once in the yard behind the café, Julia folded her arms and waited for Clive to talk.

"You really are a live wire," Clive said. "If this is

about the information, you only had to wait a few hours."

"This is about Tia. You're trying to squeeze out her last drop of passion for drumming. You can't control her like this, contracts or not."

"All Jax, I can assure you," he said, lowering his voice. "I'm just the man who brings it all together. They're the talent. I don't have the power to enforce the contracts. Jax is—"

"A creative genius?"

"A *hack*." Clive's brows arched high. "He's no more a genius than you or I, and I don't think he thinks he is either. He just knows what's expected of him. Same as Jett. You have to sell it, do you understand? I'm sure you're all smiles behind that counter even on your worst days?"

Julia couldn't deny it. On the days that she couldn't fake it, she hid in the kitchen as much as she could. She hadn't thought about how to handle those days in her rush back.

"I'm just trying to sort myself out, okay?" Clive's voice softened for the first time since he'd arrived. "I thought I was doing you a favour by agreeing to shoot the video here. There were other options, you know."

Clive arched a brow at her, and she nearly reminded him that she'd only offered because he'd been in desperate need. For the sake of the information he'd promised, she bit her tongue.

"It benefits me in no way to tell you this," he said after a sigh, looking back at the café. "I've already lost so much. But it's looking like this record deal isn't going to happen."

"You seemed so sure earlier."

"I'm trying not to spook the talent on the off chance the reps they're sending see the potential." He moved in closer and said, "I want all of this to be over as much as you do. The stress is going to kill me."

"Does this have something to do with Jax?"

Clive nodded.

"I heard you talking to him on the bench out front," he whispered, moving further from the café. "Jax *was* in Peridale on the first day of the festival."

"I've already seen proof of that."

"But you don't know why he was here. He showed up early in the morning, before any of us, and hounded me from the second he saw me."

"Hounded you about what?"

"His dismissal from the band." Clive turned Julia toward the field and spread his hands. "Tomorrow, a few hundred people might turn up for this thing. This field will swallow them. Those festival crowds don't turn up for specific acts. Some people do, but most are there for the experience. The atmosphere. You have to be able to conjure that atmosphere to get on that stage. You see where I'm going?"

"Jett could, and Jax can't?"

"Jax *thinks* he can, and that's sometimes enough to convince everyone else." Clive shrugged. "The test will be on Saturday, but given what he was asking of me on that first day, the police might have carted him away by then." Looking around again, he leaned in, and out of the side of his mouth, whispered, "He asked me to convince Jett to get rid of Tia so he could get back in the band. *Begging*, to tell you the truth. He didn't save any of their touring money, and he's knocked on every label door, without finding a scrap of work."

"Why did Jett fire him?"

"Because he wasn't able to make Jax do what he wanted. Jax had sat in the back long enough to know he wanted a taste of the spotlight. He's a desperate man, and—"

"Are we moving onto the next scene, or what?" Jax called. "I thought you were in a hurry."

"Which is why we'll have to pick this up in a few hours." Checking his watch, Clive looked at Julia and said, "Only if you don't mind us continuing to use the café? We'll be cleared by morning."

"One more thing," she asked, rushing after Clive. "Do you know if Jax drinks?"

"He's been on the wagon for years. Why?"

"No reason."

Alone behind her café, under a blanket of grey clouds, Julia pulled out her phone and looked at the picture of Mix and Jax again. With their clasped and foreheads together, they did look like they could be praying. If Jax had managed to stay sober in a rock band and Mix was struggling to do the same even with a five-year chip, maybe this was the help she'd gone to get in those ten minutes? She wished she'd asked Georgia what time she'd taken the picture.

A police car pulled up in the alley as the first drops of rain since the day of the festival hit Julia on the forehead. DI Christie hopped out and she braced for another arrest, but he went straight into the café without giving her a second look.

"Jax?" Christie called as the bell jangled. "Would you like to accompany me to the station? I'd like to ask you a few questions about your whereabouts last Friday."

As Julia crossed the green, she noticed the church doors were wide open for the first time since the electrocution.

19

*J*ulia returned to her gran's cottage expecting things to have calmed down, but they'd only grown more heated. Jessie and Percy were in the sitting room playing cards while Barker distracted Olivia at the bottom of the garden.

"What is this achieving?" Julia called during a moment of silence as Dot and Shilpa searched for comebacks. "We all want to figure out what's going on, but this won't get us there."

"It just might." Dot planted her feet. "Shilpa *still* thinks Gef is behind it after everything I've put together about Mix."

"And I said I don't care." Shilpa copied Dot on the other side of the table. "I think this is exactly what Gef wanted. He's back, and he did an interview where he said he regretted leaving music behind only two months ago. I *know* them."

"You're really no different than that girl." Dot wafted a finger at the blank board. "The only people who can even claim to have known Jett were in the village on the day he died. Gef wasn't."

"He could have been!"

"Julia?" Dot cried. "Bring some sense into the room."

"I think screaming and shouting isn't going to help." Julia pulled out a chair on either side. "I'm sure Gef's wife and three children can confirm where he was last Friday. Until then, the church is open again, so why don't we revisit the crime scene and try to put this together calmly and rationally?"

Thinking of everything Tia and Clive had told her, Julia couldn't give any attention to Dot and Shilpa's continued low-level bickering as they made their way from the dining room to the hall. If Jax had turned up in the village wanting Tia's place, why was Jett the one who'd ended up dead?

She popped her head into the sitting room. The card game had ended, and Jessie and Percy were both at the window with binoculars pressed against the glass.

"Anything interesting?"

"There's a man playing air guitar in the alley," Jessie said, not moving away. "Sort of looks like a banker on a stag night."

"That'll be Gef," Shilpa called.

"Poor fella keeps leaning against the wall. I think he's rather worked up."

"That'll be Gef's guilty conscience."

"Not this again."

"I told you, I can believe what I want, Dorothy."

Jessie and Percy glanced over their shoulders at the same time, both shaking their heads.

"Since when do those two not get along?" Jessie asked, joining Julia in the hall as Shilpa and Dot bickered by the gate. "They're like two pieces of sandpaper."

"Since they started to spend so much time together," Percy said. "Stubborn personalities. I fear our little group may be reaching its natural end. We all gave so much to save the library, but it's been difficult to get everyone together in the right moods since then. We've all been running on fumes, and your grandmother has noticed. I don't think she'll admit it, but I think she'll be glad when the burden lessens."

Percy hurried to catch up with Dot and Shilpa. They ignored his attempt to walk in the middle of them, so he forced himself between them with a wriggling behind.

"Weren't going without us, were you?" Barker shut the door before the dogs trotted out. "I remember when this case was supposed to be our little secret."

"Romantic." Jessie pulled them in closer with a wide stretch. "Most people have a date night once a week. You two solve murders."

"We haven't solved anything yet."

"Then you might want to start building your cases." She patted their shoulders and jogged ahead. "It's obvious who did it, isn't it?"

The church's scent of sweetly decaying wood and spices should have comforted Julia. But as familiar as it was, her baker's nose was too attuned to the subtleties. Metallic barbecue still lingered. Maybe it was only her imagination or the building pressure from the clouds, but it still turned her stomach.

"Before we go in," Julia whispered to Barker at the open doors of the vestibule, "I spoke to Tia and Clive, and they're both more or less pointing fingers at Jax."

"Add my finger."

"Are you certain?"

"Never until there's concrete evidence, but don't

you think he's been enjoying himself too much? Christie seems to think so too after seeing that picture. Said he was going to take him in for questioning. Judging by how easily you got Jax to confess to his lies, Christie might get a confession from him. He's like a dog with a bone right now."

"Who's a dog with a bone?" Jessie called to them from several pews down. "You know you're not whispering, right? This place amplifies everything. Who's going first?"

They gathered in the middle of the church, where the overlapping rugs had been placed on the night of the rehearsal. A circle formed around a dark scorch mark left behind on the stones. From their wrinkled noses, Julia knew she wasn't imagining the smell. Or the silence. She joined them in staring at the blackened stone.

"Horrific thing to happen to a person." Percy's pocket square dabbed at his eyes. "Inhumane."

"Cruel," Dot agreed. "Calculated."

"Dramatic," said Shilpa.

"Unnecessary," said Barker.

"Kinda cool." Jessie shrugged. "*What*? Electric guitar murder?"

Julia could feel them all looking at her, though her eyes wouldn't lift from the blackened stone.

"Confusing," she contributed. "And since you all

seem so certain about your suspects, I hope one of you can illuminate me."

"I think Shilpa should go first," Dot announced. "We'll go in order of likeliness, starting with the least."

"Which is why we're here." Shilpa glared across the circle as she cleared her throat. "But I'll rise above it and volunteer. And yes, I still think it was Gef for the same reason people think it was Jax. Gef's been out of the band the longest, so he needed to pull a huge stunt to get back. We might not know if he was here yet, but that's my vote."

"And I'll go from that and say that I think it was the manager, Clive," said Percy. "I worked with a few managers of my own back in my early magician days before I decided to manage myself. Can't trust any of them as far as you can throw them. He could have been respectful and waited until after Jett's funeral to continue the band, but he's had them back to work in a flash."

"Jax was happy to step in," Barker said, raising his hand. "So, I'll go next. I think Jax has the most to gain from this. He had a deep resentment for Jett, who kicked him out of the band, as well as a potential romantic connection to Jett's wife. He was here on the morning of the festival, months after he was kicked out. Why come back now?"

There was a grumble of agreement, and Julia

wondered if she should mention her theory about what she thought their real relationship status might be. She decided against it, wanting to hear what else they had to say.

"Jax begged Clive for Tia's place in the band," Julia said. "Clive said Jax spent the summer knocking on label doors, and he couldn't even get a job as a session drummer."

"Tia *is* the better drummer," Shilpa agreed. "And Mix is better than Gef, too. Which is why I think it was Gef who got her out of the way to clear his path back into the band."

"Still on Gef?" Dot cleared her throat. "But since you brought up the most likely candidate, I will gladly take over and explain why Vivienne Astley-Smythe, also known as Mix, killed her husband, Jett Fury, and then fled the scene like a thief in the night."

"What did she steal?" Jessie asked.

"Her husband's life." Dot clenched her fist over the scorch mark. "And I bet she wore that metal dress as her get out of jail free card in case she was accused. I wouldn't be surprised if the police were building a strong case against her, and that's why she hopped out of Peridale and halfway across the world."

"You thought that about Georgia," Julia reminded her.

"Need I remind you all that Mix is an aristocratic

socialite?" Dot searched the circle for agreement. "Even if Mummy and Daddy cut her out of the will, she probably has a friend in every port with a villa on every coast."

In the silence, Julia felt the sway.

It was a compelling theory.

"You said it was obvious," Julia said, catching Jessie's eye. "Care to share?"

"I think it was Georgia," she said. "Losing family and being made homeless is all tough. It can make people do desperate things. But the things she's done are certifiably insane. The kid was just looking for some family. And I get it, but it's insane nonetheless."

They all went back to staring at the black scorch mark.

"Something tells me her mother couldn't have picked a worse band to follow around and throw herself at." Dot didn't try to hide her judgement. "Poor mite is a victim as much as Jett. Why tell anyone she thought Jett Fury was her father once he was dead? That would only incriminate her since she was the only person of the three involved still alive to know."

"She denies that he's dead," Julia said. "Throw that into the mix."

"Is that a hint that you think *I'm* right?" Dot asked. "Mix *does* look the most likely."

Julia looked around the circle, each of them

thinking something different. She'd hoped to be swayed, but her earlier answer still hadn't changed. As big as the church was, the old stone walls were creeping in around them.

"I don't know for certain," Julia said. "But I still don't think it was Mix."

"What about Tia?" Jessie asked. "Nobody said her name, so does anyone think she did it?"

"Tia admitted to setting up the rehearsal space," Julia revealed, "but she said there was a ten-minute gap when she left things alone. Dog walkers confirmed seeing her in the graveyard, but it's still only her word that the space was set up correctly when she left it. Given how Jax treats her, she's in a much worse situation now than she was before, and for what it's worth, my gut tells me she's not involved."

"So, to clarify," Dot announced, planting her hands on her hips, "it could still be any of them?"

"Until we have more evidence, it has to be." Barker said, checking his watch. "Time for Olivia's lunch. Nothing says we must figure this out right now."

"I'll follow you out," Shilpa said. "Hopefully, the newspapers have been delivered. They're not usually this late."

"And the dogs need walking, dear." Percy hooked his arm through Dot's. "No use standing around here adding fuel to the fire. It's giving me the jitters."

When only Julia and Jessie remained, Julia paced around the mark. It was almost a perfect circle, no bigger than the paddling pool on their patio, and yet so destructive.

Cruel.

Calculated.

Julia agreed with their assessments of Jett's horrible death, regardless of how he treated people. But the question that had been niggling at her continued its tickling dance around her mind. Why the rehearsal? She almost repeated it aloud, but she agreed with *all* their assessments.

"You said it was cool," she said to Jessie.

"Not every day something like this happens."

Jessie joined Julia in pacing around the scorched stone.

"Why not a pillow over the face?"

"Impossible to even attempt to frame it as an accident."

"A fall down the stairs, then?" Julia searched for the answer. "Or like Elvis on the toilet."

"Imagine if he'd died on stage. That would have been even cooler."

"Exactly." Julia paused, her teeth dragging against her bottom lip as she tried to imagine how different that story would have been. "But Elvis was already a legend, and Jett Fury was—"

"F list," Jessie said. "I've checked his socials. Aside from his lyrics and posting pictures of himself on stage, he has nothing to say about anything. He does have fans, though. I think I found Georgia's profile, unless he has several stalkers."

"Can I see?"

Jessie dug out her phone, and Julia's guilt writhed again at the mention of Georgia's name.

"Okay, so it's definitely her." Jessie flashed the phone at Julia and scrolled before her eyes had a chance to settle. "Last thing she posted before her arrest was a video of her singing an Electric Fury song in the woods. The police must have released her sometime in the last two hours because she's been posting nonstop, and they're all crazy."

Jessie stopped scrolling long enough for Julia to read the stream of messages, though she only needed to read one. They were all the same.

'JETT FURY IS ALIVE'

'JETT FURY IS ALIVE'

'JETT FURY IS ALIVE'

"I know what you're thinking," Jessie said, pulling the phone away, "but just because she told the truth about Jett being her dad doesn't mean this is true."

But could it be true?

"Mum?"

"It's a powerful idea."

Staring off into the nothingness of the church, something shiny and plastic caught her eye. She let it pull her in, and on closer inspection. She discovered that it was the new fuse box. Crouching, she noticed that the traces of superglue hadn't been lifted from the stone slabs below. She ran her fingers over the rough texture, imagining someone squirting the glue all over the switches in those ten minutes, knowing they were about to kill Jett Fury.

Ten minutes to set up a murder.

"Mum..." Jessie's voice echoed around the church. "You'll never guess what's trending."

"In Peridale?"

"In the *country*." Jessie's eyes widened as they scanned the screen. "Forget Jett being alive. *Mix* is alive."

"They've found her?"

Dot barged through the doors, flapping a newspaper. She rushed down the aisle and slapped it cover side up on the pew. With only a short headline and a single image, it was one of the more straightforward covers she'd seen, but the three words chosen had all the necessary impact:

*SOCIALITE'S **SHOCKING** CONFESSION*

"I *told* you!" Dot cried between breaths. "It was Mix all along."

The image was a handwritten note, the calligraphy perfect.

Julia picked up the paper and read:

I, Vivienne Astley-Smythe, do hereby confess to the murder of Jett Fury. I electrocuted him for his mistreatment of me during our marriage, and I'd do it again. I wish you luck trying to find me, but I'm already in paradise.

"A clear, concise confession." Dot rocked back on her heels. "She sent the note to every major publication in the country. It's national headline news. And before you claim forgery, turn to page three for the direct quote from the handwriting specialist. Her parents were more than happy to provide years of samples."

Julia read over the confession again.

"Mum?"

"Looks like I saved you a job when I wiped the board, Gran. Our investigation is over."

20

*S*itting on the scratched-up counter with her legs dangling over the edge, Julia stared at the rolled-down blind as the rain lashed behind it. She waited to be hit by the wave of relief that *The Peridale Post*'s shocking headline had washed over the village. She'd gladly have taken a drop, but she couldn't stop reading over the confession.

Clear.

Concise.

Very Astley-Smythe.

"You can't be right every time, Julia," her gran had said before Julia had locked herself in the café. "And don't feel sorry for her. She had you thinking she was missing, after all. Be glad it's over."

"I want to be."

Abandoning the paper, Julia looked at the first times box. She'd brought it out as soon as she'd walked across the café now thankfully free of equipment and the antique chair. She reached to the bottom and pulled out the framed picture.

"Took a guess and went for fish and chips," Jessie called, coming in through the back door. "I can't believe they're still at the window. You think they'd take the blinds as a hint."

Julia counted three people with their hands cupped against the glass. She'd seen them coming and going from the corner of her eye for as long as it had been pouring down, but she hadn't been able to face them. They were looking for somewhere to talk about the scandalous headline, and Julia's Café didn't have a table, chair, or even plate to serve on.

"I saw a place in Germany that looked sort of like this," Jessie said, dropping the food on the counter. "The right lighting, and it's industrial-chic."

"I don't think it's quite Peridale."

"No, you're probably right." Propping her hand up like she was holding an invisible tray, Jessie weaved in and out of tables that weren't there. "Yes, the weather *is* delightful, Amy, and while I agree it's *delicious*, Father David, we sold the last slice of lemon drizzle cake not thirty minutes ago. What's that, Ethel? You think your cappuccino is *four* degrees too hot? I'd be *honoured* to pour it down the drain and make you another one."

Julia laughed, and the smile lingered – Jessie's intention, no doubt.

She looked down at the framed picture in her hands, and the smile faded. She was six years younger in the photograph, wearing a pink apron and standing under her café's first sign. The sign had changed, the inside had been redecorated, and Julia couldn't believe how much younger she looked. The only thing that wasn't her was the pose.

"Sue was behind the camera with my gran," Julia explained. "She told me to 'power pose', and all I could come up with was planting my hands on my hips. I was so raring to go. So ready for the future, even though I had no idea if it would work. Barely had the money to do it, either, but I did it anyway."

"It's a lovely story," Jessie said, unfolding the paper-wrapped chips. "One you usually tell a little lighter."

"I'm standing in the ruin of *her* dream."

"Is that how you really feel?"

Staring at the picture, Julia nodded. She was sure if she'd stood there as long on the morning Jax had interrupted her, she'd have come to the same conclusion.

"Used to be a phone shop," she said, looking around. "Sat empty for three years. They still had the display models out all along this wall." She walked over to the wall where the postcards had hung, the wallpaper peeking through in stencilled rectangles. "The popcorn, Jett's murder ... it's all been one giant distraction from the fact I don't think I was truly ready to come back. Not on my own. But I didn't know what else to do. I panicked and reset to default."

"No offence, Mum, but your default has always been to try and keep every plate spinning on your own. I'm back now. You don't have to figure everything out at once. When we started travelling, I let the constant airports and long journeys stress me out. I was homesick too, but Alfie told me I was only stressed because I was thinking about everything all at once. Plane, bus, hotel, plane, bus, hotel."

"It does sound stressful."

"Café, mother, wife, neighbourhood watch..." Julia could see where she was going. "When we were in Japan, we went to this gorgeous temple. It was mostly full of tourists, but there were real monks there. I was sitting on a step, waiting for Alfie to stop chatting up this woman, and I knew I was ready to come back. I knew I'd seen enough, done enough, but I couldn't face it. Felt like a failure not to do the full year."

"You're never a failure."

"I know, but that's how I felt at *that* moment." She shrugged. "Like you are now, I was down on myself. Unprompted, one of the monks came over, and asked what was troubling me. I guess it was obvious from my face that I had the weight of the world on my shoulders. He said something simple. He said, 'Flow like water', and I probably looked as confused as you, so I asked what he meant. I'm going to butcher this, but it was something like, if water stands still, you can see the dust settle, and when it's moving, it can go in any direction. It'll always adapt to whatever it comes across. You sit around and focus on the dust for too long, life's going to look a bit rubbish, isn't it? You just have to keep moving and look for the positive in the negative. My negative was that I felt like a failure for wanting to cut the trip short, but the positive was that I could come home and see all the people I loved. You came back because you were ready to, even if you weren't sure. The stream might have changed direction and covered that direction in graffiti, but positives will still come out of this."

"Like a new café?"

"Exactly." Jessie winked. "And you get to show that woman in the picture what you can do with this place now. She hasn't gone anywhere. Who cares if you didn't solve this case?"

"I'm not upset I wasn't the one to solve it." Julia looked at the paper again, unsure of what she felt. "I'm sorry, Jessie. I feel like I've barely asked you anything about your travels, and you clearly have a lot to share."

"I'm glad you didn't ask everything at once," Jessie said quickly. "I needed a few days to adjust. I thought I'd be doing them working here, but I think I've acclimatised, and my timing couldn't have been more perfect."

"Did your dad—"

"Nobody told me to come home." Jessie stepped into the middle of the café and spun around. "I thought I was going to upset Alfie, but he reminded me of what he'd told me to stop me feeling homesick in those early days. I'd know when I was ready, so I should stop waiting for it to happen. I had the time of my life, but I was ready for home. That night I rushed off the phone when I wouldn't turn my camera on, I had twenty minutes to decide if I wanted to get on the first plane home. I only had to hear your voice for twenty seconds to know I was ready. Like Georgia, I spent enough of my life looking for a home to know I had one to return to."

"And Alfie?"

"The world is his home, and he'll be back when he's ready, and he isn't. I've learned so much, lived so much, I wish I could just..." Jessie held her fingers on either side of Julia's head and pushed her temples. "But there's no rush. Right now, we need to figure out how to put this place right, though I'm sure people would come in regardless of how it looks. Phone shop, café ... it's just a building. Your listening ear and passion for baking put the spark in this place."

"You think?"

"I know." Jessie gave her a comforting hug. "This café is the watering hole in paradise to many people around here. Now, should we take these across to Dot's? I saw Evelyn and Amy go in on my way. Would be a shame to waste all these chips."

Jessie put the uneaten food back in the plastic bag, uncovering the newspaper front page again. Folded at the top, only the bottom of the note was visible. Julia read over it, one word snagging like it hadn't on her previous reads.

"What did you *just* say?"

"Flow like water?"

"Something about paradise?"

"Oh, it's just something we'd joke about." Jessie laughed, opening the café's front door. "Alfie knows a lot of people from all walks of life, so sometimes it was luxury apartments. Most of the time, it was hostels, sofas, and the odd bus station. No matter where we were, we'd look for the good. He'd say that anywhere could be paradise if you looked closely enough."

Taking the chips with her, Jessie hurried through the rain in the direction of Dot's cottage, and taking the paper with her, Julia was hot on her heels. In the sitting room, she was surprised to see all members of Peridale's Ears, including Johnny and Amy. They hadn't been seen since before the festival.

"Ah, Julia," Dot said with a sombre sigh. "That makes it a full house. We've all been talking, and we've decided—"

"I think Mix is in Peridale."

"What?" Dot sprung to life. "She said she'd run off."

"No, she said she was in paradise." Julia was out of breath, her mind racing. Was she jumping to the conclusion that wasn't there? "When she left the nail salon, she said this place was as good as paradise, and I agreed. I think she's trying to send me a message."

"Why would she do that?" Dot cried. "This is absurd!"

"Because I don't think she killed Jett."

"The confession is printed right there."

Dot dragged the paper from Julia's hands, her touch as dry as sandpaper.

"Your hands..."

"It's super glue," she said, exhaling as she scanned the room. "*Someone* broke my drone, and *nobody* is admitting to it. It was messy, but I fixed it."

Dry hands.

Super glue.

"I think I know who is behind all of this."

21

"*J*ulia, *enough!*" Christie slapped down the newspaper on the interview table. "You're basing all of this on a cryptic feeling."

"A conversation."

"That you have no evidence of."

"Isn't my statement evidence?"

"You've already given a statement, and you failed to mention anything about paradise."

"Because it was a passing comment." Julia turned the newspaper to him. "Look at how she wrote it. The first two sentences are overly formal, and then the last two looser, like somebody else wrote them."

"The handwriting specialist has already confirmed it was written by her." Christie opened a folder and spread photocopied sheets across the desk. "All the way back to her private education days. *She* wrote it."

"Probably under duress from whoever has been keeping her for these last few days." Julia took a calming breath. "John, I think she is sending me a message."

"Why *you*, Julia?"

"I don't know, but she opened up to me." Julia reached across the table and picked up one of the samples. A school report, the first comment of which was 'Vivienne must try harder with her etiquette and diction.' "She told me about her parents, how much she hated being like them. This sounds like they wrote it."

"But only the first two lines?" He laughed. "So, now you're saying her parents are behind this?"

Julia wasn't sure what she was saying. She read the lines over again, the over formality just as jarring.

"No," she said, tapping the paper with a finger. "But maybe it sounds like what someone *thinks* a person like Vivienne sounds like. They could have been feeding her lines to get her to confess. Maybe she free-styled the last two? This could have said anything, but she *chose* the word 'paradise.'"

"Have you considered that she's messing with you?" he asked, and she shook her head. "Another sick game? If she did kill him, that's pretty twisted, Julia. You spoke to her. She's a handful. Remember, she tried to have you banged up for leaving a notepad behind."

"I never said she was perfect."

"Are you sure about this?"

"Are you ever completely sure?" she asked. "She could have picked any word."

Christie groaned as he dragged the newspaper off the table. In his hurry, he knocked the samples on the floor. He was barking orders to have the village searched again, but Julia was focused on the report on the floor next to her. The only teacher who had bothered to write extensively was her English teacher, whose name Julia couldn't quite make out in the scrawl. But the final line of her report had been underlined.

'If Vivienne applies herself, she could be our nation's next great poet. Unfortunately, she does not.'

The report wasn't Julia's, and the words still stung.

Her teacher wanted her to be a poet.

Her parents wanted her to be like them.

Her husband wanted her to stand in the back.

Lost in the Mix, Vivienne just wanted to be heard, and she was screaming.

"I'm listening," Julia said. "C'mon, Mix. Tell me where you are."

"Nothing," Barker said with tight lips as he placed the peppermint and liquorice tea in front of her. "They've gone over every inch."

"You know they can't have gone over *every* inch."

"I know." He rubbed the back of her hand. "But they're really trying. What's this?"

"Latest notes. Hadn't had a chance to write them down."

"Jett Fury is alive?" Barker hesitated at the curtains. "I didn't have you down as a conspiracy theorist."

"It's what Georgia thinks."

"Is it what you think?"

Julia sipped her tea as he turned off the lamp on the sideboard.

"No. But it's a powerful idea. I think we can use it."

"Use it for what?" Barker yawned. "I was only on my way to the bathroom. Are you coming to bed?"

Another sip, but the pen didn't stop.

"Soon. I think I have a plan to smoke them out." Julia smiled over the top of her cup. "How would you like to go on a date tomorrow night? I can't promise the band will be any good, but I think I can get us tickets to a show."

The next evening, standing at the bedroom window in Jessie's flat, Julia waited with bated breath as she checked between the bulky black pair and the tiny plastic pair of binoculars.

"I can see the stage with these ones." She tossed the black pair onto the bed next to the drone. "The lighter, the better. I can't believe she had so many to choose from."

"A pair at every window."

"Isn't she creeping the neighbours out?"

"I hope so, because maybe then I won't have to tell her I'm quitting."

"For real?"

"One less thing to flow around."

Jessie left the window and walked over to the bed. She picked up her phone, and with a few taps, the drone hovered a couple of inches.

"I've seen too many videos of these things crashing," said Julia.

"Then you spend more time on your phone than I do." Jessie glanced up at her with a dry smile. "I only need to hover. Look, I've already mastered..."

With a nudge of her thumb, the drone shot sideways into the pillow.

"Learning curve. How'd you get Georgia to agree to do this, anyway?"

"Practically bit my hand off. She's been waiting for her chance to be heard."

"You've given her a big stage to do it on."

"You should have seen the one last week." Julia headed to the door. "Good luck."

"Don't panic," Jessie called back. "What could possibly go wrong?"

Julia brushed down the crease in her vintage yellow dress and shook out her curls. She dragged on mauve lipstick, her 'perfect' shade according to the quiz Sue had sat her through long ago. Almost as long since she'd used it. She rubbed her lips together and blended in the crumbly bits.

Barker appeared behind her in the mirror, looping up his tie.

"Look at us," she said. "If you squint and ignore the piles of baby clothes on the bed, we look like we did when we first met."

"We had more time to make an effort." He slipped his hands around her waist. "Sue should be here soon. Should we go over the plan again?"

"We know what we're doing." She kissed him and

rubbed off the lipstick before blending the excess into her cheeks. "Everything's already in place. We just need to sit back and watch the show."

"Almost like a real date."

"Aren't you having fun?"

"The most I've had in a while." He nuzzled at her neck. "I love it when you talk investigations."

"Easy, Mr Brown. We need to stay focused tonight." The doorbell rang down the hall. "That'll be Sue to babysit. Time to go."

22

*J*ulia and Barker walked to the village, where Shilpa and Evelyn were waiting on the corner. Around the green, fewer people were gathered than at any moment of the festival. Through the steady flow making their way down the alley, she could see the stage through the sparse crowd.

"They moved the whole thing halfway up the field this afternoon," Shilpa said. "I thought the news of Gef returning would have drawn a bigger crowd. There's barely any atmosphere. And *that* isn't helping."

Julia assumed *that* was the music coming from the village hall, if the hesitant plucks and key hopping humming could be called music. Clive was pacing in front of the hall, puffing a cigar, though unlike the night of the festival, he didn't look like he had much reason to celebrate.

Jessie saluted from the window of her flat, and Julia returned it.

They walked down the alley with the light trickle of darkly dressed fans. There were a couple of differently branded beer cans in people's hands here and there, but the promise of a free concert didn't seem exciting for any of them.

"There's a cynical energy in the breeze tonight," said Evelyn. "Nothing has been the same since that band came here."

"Hopefully, after tonight," Julia whispered, slowing as they came to the back of the crowd, "things will go back to normal. Did you ever get paid for them staying in the flat?"

Shilpa shook her head.

"I didn't get a penny from Tia staying at the B&B either," said Evelyn. "The band's card bounced."

"And I got nothing for the video shoot. Keep your eyes peeled, girls."

The music video shot in the café played from a projector against a white sheet. It was probably for the best that the picture quality wasn't clear as the sheet fluttered in the breeze. All the smoke and lighting tricks in the world couldn't disguise that it had been recorded on a phone. With Jax's electronically drenched vocal stylings on top, Julia wasn't surprised people were laughing.

It didn't take long for the band to arrive with Clive, who quickly turned off the projector after glancing at the indifferent crowd. Tia sat behind her drums while Jax and Gef adjusted their microphones. Neither man acknowledged the gathering, their hands shaking as they fiddled to get the stands at the correct height.

"How are the grandkids, Gef?"

"This is ridiculous!"

"An insult to Jett's memory."

"He isn't even in the ground yet."

Someone hurled a can, spinning entrails of beer over the right side of the crowd. The can struck Clive's stomach. Cheering quickly replaced the groaning as an empty water bottle came from the other side, bouncing off his temple.

"Alright, alright!" Clive thudded a finger on the microphone, ducking as another can flew at him. "It's great that you're all so passionate. Nothing but some good ol' fashioned rock'n'roll. Like the good ol' days, right?"

The grumbling crowd seemed to settle a little. Behind Clive, Gef and Jax had finished plugging in their mics. Tia was scanning the crowd, and her eyes doubled to Julia, making her glad she'd worn yellow.

"The old days aren't always better, are they?" Clive called out. "Who here wishes they could have bought a Jett Fury CD?"

Clive held the microphone to the crowd, and there were some cheers.

"Or even just have been able to stream a song on your phone. Most of you, right?"

More cheers.

"I know you all miss Jett," Clive said solemnly. "I do too, every second, but that's why we're all here, isn't it? To celebrate Jett's legacy after what our former bassist did to him."

The cheering turned to booing, confirming that the fans had been just as ready to accept the confession as the rest of the village.

"But what if I said the legacy he started didn't have to end?" Clive called. "Before Jett's passing, we were working on something special for you all. But like with the return of Gef...' Clive turned to him, and Gef looked like he wanted to be anywhere but on the stage. 'Can we get a round of applause for the return of the band's *original* bassist?"

Tepid applause rippled quickly through the crowd.

"There's no denying the band is in a bad place," Clive said with a sigh as he looked out into the crowd.

He scanned right past Julia. "But does that mean it needs to be over when there's still so much to do?"

"Get on with it!" someone cried as a crushed can struck one of Tia's cymbals.

"The people are ready," Clive said, turning to the band. "Which makes me even more excited to announce that for the first time in the history of this amazing band, their music, including their entire back catalogue, is available for recording. So, if you want all those songs you know and love at home, I will need you to go crazy and lose your minds for the new and improved *Electric Fury*!"

"Are you all ready?" Jax called through his microphone. "*Let's go!*"

Tia activated, her drumming leading them in. From Jax's first strum, his lack of confidence poured out. Gef seemed just as shy, but at least his playing sounded like it went with the drumming. Julia wasn't sure if Jax could hear how jarring his hesitant strumming was. Behind clenched eyes, he sang monotonously through screwed-up lips crammed against the mic. Every breath and brush of his lips crackled painfully through the speakers. Gef's eyes were on Tia while she scanned the crowd, who'd stopped cheering and had taken to staring in what felt like a shocked silence.

"Am I missing something, Shilpa?" Evelyn whispered.

"This is the worst Electric Fury show I've ever been to," she replied with a groan. "I'm not sure I want to see this. I think my nostalgia-tinted glasses just shattered."

And she wasn't alone.

People were already turning their backs and walking away.

On the stage, Tia's eyes met Julia's desperately as she continued to drum. Jax gained confidence, turning his mutter-singing into near-screaming. Tia's eyes flicked up above Julia's head. Julia resisted doing the same to avoid drawing attention, instead listening out for the soft whirring. Barker's hand slipped around hers and squeezed. He heard it too.

"Don't worry, Shilpa," Julia said. "You're about to be put out of your misery."

If Jax had opened his eyes, he might have seen Georgia stumbling onto the stage. She fell to her knees in front of the drums as Clive yanked her back with her hood. After staggering into the drums, Georgia unzipped her hoody and launched herself at Jax's microphone stand.

Before she snatched it up, sirens turned Julia around. She looked between Shilpa and Evelyn, still transfixed by what was happening on the stage, as multiple police cars zoomed down the alley.

"*Mix is in the village!*" Georgia cried. "She's *here*! She's—"

Georgia continued to scream as Jax tugged the microphone. Even if anyone could hear her over the confused chatter, the sirens drawing closer overwhelmed the rest. Police cars skidded in a semi-circle behind them.

"This is an *illegal* gathering!" Christie cried through a megaphone. "Nobody move, you're all under arrest."

"What do we do?" Julia asked Barker.

"We *run*!" Evelyn replied. "I've been to enough illegal raves to know they can't catch us all!"

Evelyn and Shilpa were gone in a flash, leaving Julia and Barker caught in opposite streams as people rushed to evade the officers closing in. They already had people on the ground and in cuffs. Barker's hand tightened around hers, and they sprinted.

"Did you see where he ran to?"

"I saw Jax heading back towards the green, but not the others."

Wondering if it had all been for nothing, Julia searched the skies for the drone. She couldn't see it, but that wasn't necessarily a bad thing. Running wide around the field, they approached the back of the post office, and after waiting for another car full of officers to empty, they darted across the alley and into the café's yard.

"Scare tactics," Barker said. "Evelyn was right, they can't arrest everyone, and they'll only release them tomorrow…"

Barker tapped Julia's shoulder and pointed to the shoes sticking out between the plastic and cardboard recycling bins.

"She won't have heard us," Julia said, stepping forward. Tia was hunched over, head down, rocking. "Barker, kick the bucket."

"I'm sorry?"

"The mop bucket."

Barker gave it a kick and it crashed like a cymbal around the yard. Tia's head shot up, and her worried eyes softened at the sight of Julia.

"What did Georgia say?" Tia asked as Julia helped her up. "I didn't see."

"I asked her to claim she'd seen Mix in the village."

"Didn't she?"

"No." She apologised with a smile. "But I think she is, and the only person who wouldn't believe she'd been seen was whoever took Mix. I hoped Clive would lead us to—"

Julia heard something that sent her climbing onto

a milk crate. Over the wall, the crowd had thinned to a few brave stranglers still launching whatever they could as the police pushed them further out. DI Christie was leaning against the back of the post office, vaping white clouds while, the officers bundled the handcuffed into vans. He seemed to be resisting rubbing his hands together. There'd be no getting through to him until they had something concrete.

"Mum?" Jessie whispered. She was at her bedroom window, also looking down at Christie. She put her fingers up to her ear, which was the sign for Julia to look at her phone.

A video from Jessie.

As Julia had hoped, the 'good pixels' Percy had promised showed the stage as clear as day, even at night. Georgia grabbed the microphone, and Julia saw the reaction the police had distracted her from.

Clive had a look of sheer panic on his face.

He set off running.

The drone followed him all the way to the edge of Howarth Forest before the signal faded, ending the video.

"Clive's been trying to capture lightning in a bottle," she said, pulling open the gate. "Now, let's go and see where he's been keeping his hostage."

23

*S*ticking close to the shadows, they hurried towards Howarth Forest, leaving the café and the police behind.

"I don't think we'll have much time," Julia said, catching up with Tia, who was leading the charge. "Of all the people accused of going on the run lately, Clive is the one I can see fleeing to the airport before the encore. But considering his IOU attitude, I'm not sure Clive can afford a plane ticket right now."

"I think you're right, and I think he's been rinsing the band's accounts too," said Tia. "I haven't been paid for any work since Jett died."

Ignoring the path cutting across from the green to the school, Julia climbed over the low stone wall and helped Tia to the other side. Weaving through the gravestones, following the same path the drone had, they reached the dark edge of Howarth Forest. The trees swallowed them up in a gulp of cooling air, bringing a chill across Julia's arms.

"Now where?" Barker's voice was low as he moved in close to Julia. "This forest goes on for miles in every direction."

A stone's throw away, Tia stopped in a clearing. She crouched, her fingers touching the ground. Straining her eyes, she tilted her head as they joined her.

"Can you hear an engine?"

"No." Barker replied immediately. "Can't hear a thing."

Julia joined Tia in crouching and rested her fingers against the soil. She couldn't hear an engine, but there was a light tickling in her fingers. Like a radio shifting stations, the low hum of an engine faded in and out. Giving up on her ears, she focused on her fingers, and her head suddenly tilted to a constant rumbling sound.

"You hear it," Tia stated, a smile spreading. A bang somewhere off in the forest made Tia's fingers pull back. "What was that?"

"Sounded like a car door slamming," Barker replied, pointing left. "I think it came from that direction."

"No." Tia shook her head and pushed herself up. "This way."

Taking more careful steps, Tia crept away from the clearing in the opposite direction Barker had pointed. Julia had heard somewhere between, so she followed Tia despite Barker's worried expression.

Ahead, Tia stopped and crouched again. Only her fingers weren't on the ground this time. She waved them over and motioned for them to get low. Pointing at her eyes, she gestured up ahead.

Julia crouched next to her and realised that *ahead* actually meant *below*. Large trees loomed all around a cliff-like ridge, their thick roots keeping the rest of the ground from crumbling away. In the middle, the ashes of a campfire, but Tia's eyes were fixed further ahead. Julia squinted towards an orange glow lighting up the darkness in the shadow of an oak tree as tall as the church spire.

At first, she thought it was a firefly.

And then she saw the smoke.

The glow returned, brighter, casting some light against the shiny black glass of the tour bus Clive was leaning against. It almost blended in with the shadows.

"He told me it had been picked up," Julia mouthed to Tia. "Said it was for the festival season."

"Jett's had it for years," she mouthed back. "He told *me* it had gone for its yearly service."

"So, why did he bring it here?" Barker whispered, edging closer and nodding down to the burnt-out campfire surrounded by litter. "Do you think they've been living here?"

"At least since Mix went missing."

Clive moved away from the van. The trail of smoke drifted behind him as he walked toward them. Holding her breath, Julia waited for him to look up and see her bright yellow dress, but he sat by the fire. After squirting what she assumed was lighter fluid, he held his cigar against some paper and tossed it in. The campfire went up in a blaze that made him chuckle.

"Maybe we confront him?" Barker suggested. "He might confess."

"Do you really think he would?" Julia asked.

Barker shook his head.

"We could be here all—"

Barker didn't finish his sentence.

All of them, including Clive, snapped their heads in the direction of rustling in the bushes behind the bus. Still puffing his cigar, Clive picked up a tree branch and set off towards the sound.

"Could have been a stray cat," Barker whispered, patting Julia on the shoulder. "Or maybe we're not alone. Stay here and keep watch."

"No." Tia replied. "We came here to get evidence against that pig, and that's what we're going to do. If he killed Jett and has Mix, this ends tonight."

Still crouched, Tia followed the curve of the land. Julia didn't want to leave either of them, but Barker had police training to protect him. She gave him a quick kiss and hurried after the drummer. She caught up as Tia was kicking rubbish around the fire. Like the festival field, it was mainly crushed beer cans and empty crisp packets, with extra cigar butts thrown in.

Tia was already on her way to the bus, but something blue on the edge of the flames caught Julia's eye. A scorched picture of a woman grinned up at her from behind a window of bubbled plastic with blackened edges. The half of her face not burned away had perfect skin and a not so perfect looking shiny wig.

A blue wig.

An electric blue wig.

"Framing a child, Clive?" she whispered, looking up at the quiet bushes and hoping Barker was safe.

Tia had already given up on the locked door of the bus. Julia cupped her hands against the glass, remembering how she hadn't been able to see her father inside when he'd called to her. The lights were off, but Julia and Tia couldn't have gone unseen if someone had been onboard.

"Here," Tia whispered, and Julia hurried around the bus. "I can fit through there. Jett locked the keys inside on our Lincoln date."

Tia climbed onto the passenger seat and pulled open a small wooden door in the wall between the cabin and the central part of the bus. It only seemed big enough to fit a cake through. With a bit of twisting, Tia fed herself to the other side. She landed with a thud, jolting the bus.

Kneeling on the passenger seat, Julia looked through. The inside was even more of a mess. From the looks of the bundles of sheets Tia was digging through, at least two people were sleeping on the sofas. Papers were spread across the table, and unless Jax had started writing his vision in long form, Julia was sure she was looking at the contracts.

"Tia?" Julia whispered through the hatch. "Open the door and let me onboard."

But Tia didn't turn around. She continued down the bus, searching among more stacks of papers in a mess on the kitchen counter, before making her way to the recording booth at the back end. She crouched under the console full of dials and knobs and rifled through the boxes underneath.

"Tia?"

Tia stood up and looked through the window into the booth. She stood there for a moment, and Julia scanned around her. The forest was too quiet. So quiet she jumped when her phone buzzed in her dress pocket. She pulled it out.

An image received via Air from Georgia Kingsley.

Again?

Julia tapped on it, surprised to see the tour bus she was currently on, and it looked like it had been taken from the same angle Julia and Tia had been looking down from only moments ago.

"Mix?" Tia cried. "*Mix!*"

"Tia?"

Julia's fingers clung to the edge of the hatch as Tia fumbled with the recording studio door. Suddenly, a head of blonde hair popped up, and two black-ringed eyes stared out, straight at Julia. Mix's palms beat down on the glass as Tia fought with the door, and from her open jaw, she was screaming in the soundproof booth.

Julia looked down at the picture again.

What was Georgia trying to tell her?

With the blazing fire, the clearing wasn't so dark anymore. Light enough to see the hooded figure sitting on the wooden logs. Julia twisted her head and looked in the fire's direction, but they'd gone.

Tia hadn't stopped screaming for Mix.

The door unclicked from the outside.

Frozen in the passenger seat, Julia's jaw slackened

as she watched the hooded figure climb aboard. Mix stopped her silent screaming. She slammed her palms down, trying to catch Tia's attention.

"Stop!" Julia cried. "Don't lay a finger on her."

The hooded figure stopped and dropped their head to the side. Julia didn't need to see their face to know who it was, only their green hair.

"Jax, don't hurt her."

But Julia's words were going unheard by everyone.

Copying Mix, Julia hit the metal partition wall with the heel of her palm. Tia's head jerked up, and she ducked as Jax lunged for her. His hood flew down, and ignoring Mix, he grabbed at Tia and tossed her down to the ground. Julia left the passenger seat and ran around the bus and through the open door. She stood between Jax and Tia, her eyes going to the blade she hadn't realised he was holding in her panic.

"This has gone far enough," she said, taking a step closer to Tia. "Clive put you up to this? Something tells me you didn't pull it off alone."

"What's that supposed to mean?" Jax cried before swinging around and pointing the knife at Mix through the window. "Why couldn't you just go along with it? We were supposed to be getting signed tonight."

"Did you believe that, Jax?" asked Julia.

"It was *my* time."

"But did you *really* believe you could pull it off?"

"What?" Jax repositioned himself and held the knife further out. "Why do you keep getting involved? This was never about *you*. In fact, if you hadn't kept sticking your nose in, we wouldn't be in this mess. I did everything he asked of me. Jett kicked me out, so I went away and waited. Clive promised me *everything*!"

"Oh, Jax." Julia sighed. "You were convincing him as much as he was convincing you. Did you think you could just pick up Jett's guitar and take over the band?"

"I can!"

"The fans saw different tonight."

"If they hadn't been throwing things..." Jax stared at the floor. "The speakers were too loud. And Clive was putting p-pressure on me all day. And I *deserve* this! This was—"

"Your time?" Julia held out her hand for the knife. "I think your time is up, Jax."

"No!"

"Not just in the band," she said, stepping closer, "but doing Clive's bidding. We both know you weren't behind any of this. Not really. That picture of you and Mix – you *were* praying, weren't you? How many years is on your chip?"

His fingers clenched around the knife.

"Ten."

"Impressive." She held out her hand further. "That can't have been easy. You were helping Mix stay on track while you were in the band, weren't you?"

"What did it matter?" He pointed the knife in Mix's direction. Mix was staring, but Julia was sure she couldn't hear what was being said. "All the help I gave her, all the counselling and advice, keeping her on the straight and narrow, it was useless. The day of the festival, she was begging for my help because she'd lost her sober babysitter, but what did *she* ever do to help *me*? She let Jett fire me."

"I don't think she could have stopped him even if she'd wanted to."

"She could have tried!" Tears welled in his eyes as red eyeliner leaked adown in bloody lines. "All those years in the band were a waste. I walked away with nothing. There was no point to any of it."

"You can still walk away from this." Julia took a step back, giving him a clear path to the door. "It won't be long until my husband returns with the police. If you go now, you might still be able to get away. This isn't you. The real you. *This* is all Clive."

Jax only needed to take a moment to think about it.

The knife clattered on the floor before he bombed down the bus's stairs. Kicking the knife away, Julia helped Tia up, noticing a cluster of keys atop the table of contracts. Even if Jax ran straight to the airport, she was sure he wouldn't get far with such striking hair.

Her sympathy had gone as far as getting them away from the knife. Jax might only have been a puppet, but he'd gone along with everything gladly for his own gain. She didn't care what happened to him next.

Filtering through smaller keys with trembling hands, she tried four before the padlock unclicked. She opened the door, and Tia squeezed past into Mix's arms. The recording booth was slightly bigger than a bathtub; just big enough for a sleeping bag, a pallet of bottled water, and a pile of protein bars.

"Took you long enough," Mix said, pulling Julia tight. "And here I was starting to think you didn't get my message."

24

$\mathcal{M}$ix wasted no time running off the bus. She crouched low and didn't stop until her forehead was resting on the ground. Once there, she started sobbing. Julia rubbed her back as the sobs turned to shoulder-heaving laughs.

"You don't realise how different the ground feels until you're hovering just above it with nothing but your thoughts all day," she said through her choked chuckles. "I thought I was going to die in there."

"We need to get you to the hospital," said Julia as Mix stood up and stared bright-eyed at the sky. "And we can call the police from there."

"Do they think I did it?"

"They won't when we talk to them."

"I don't need to go to a hospital," Mix said, tossing

her hands out as she jogged backwards. "Like I said, nothing but my thoughts. Cheaper than rehab, not that I could afford it anyway. Best I've felt in years."

Mix started jogging the way they'd come, and Tia ran after her. Looking back at the bus and the bushes, Julia listened for Barker. Nothing. Had the rustling been Georgia? Forcing down the lump in her throat, she had to trust that her husband knew what he was doing. She set off at a run, looking back at the bus one last time. She couldn't fathom how she'd act in a similar situation. Still, she might have started running as far away from it too.

On their way past the ridge, she paused at the place where Georgia would have sent the picture. The guilt bubbled up fresh. She'd assumed the girl was nothing more than attention seeker, and yet she'd tried to warn Julia about Jax being at the campsite. Her phone shone up from the grass, the screen cracked. She could almost see Clive driving his heel down onto it.

"Georgia?" she called out into the silence.

No response came, so she caught up with Mix and Tia, already nearing the forest edge.

"It was all Clive," Mix called over her shoulder. "This has all been about him getting his hands on Jett's music, but if you've come this far, you've figured that out."

"What happened that night?" Julia was glad they slowed down as they came to the field. "Something tells me that you found something in the contracts?'

"You really are always paying attention." Mix twisted her arm to show the cut that must have caused the blood trickle. Even with a scab, it looked like it had been deep. "Clive read an old contract that Jett wrote in the early days that stated in the event of the death of any member, the rights to the songs would default to the founding members. Not me or Tia, only Jax and Gef. He thought with Jett out the way, he could plug Jax in and get that record deal Jett has been refusing ever since Clive showed up. I should have known that's what he was doing when he convinced Jett to replace the beds with the recording booth after the fire, but he still didn't want anything to do with it. Problem was, Clive didn't know Jett had written a newer contract, and boy, did he not like it when I showed it to him."

"What did it say?"

"That in the event of Jett's death, all the rights would go to his next of kin. Me." Mix stared up at the sky. "I think he knew Clive was going to pull a stunt. He only wrote it two weeks ago. When I showed that *pig*, his reaction told me he was behind everything. And if I hadn't gone through that bottle of wine, I might have been able to fight him off. Once I was tied up, he passed me through the window to Jax, locked me in that bus, and drove away. He's been moving me around the forest every few hours."

Explained where Clive kept running off to.

"How haven't you gone mad?" Tia asked.

"I did." Mix picked up the pace, still looking at Tia. "And then I found myself. And then I went mad again. They pretended like they couldn't see me. Couldn't hear me. But I knew they'd keep me alive. He was trying to get me to sign everything over in case Jett made copies. When I wouldn't, the next best thing was the confession to cover his back."

Mix helped Tia over the wall before nodding to Dot's cottage. "That's your grandmother's, isn't it? All that binocular watching, and she missed the one thing going on. You think she'll mind if I use her shower?"

Mix was already at the green when Julia's feet hit the stony path. Her gran, Percy, and Jessie were all waiting by the front door.

"Percy, call the police!"

"So, people *do* think I did it." Mix sighed, squeezing past. "I hope your water pressure is better than at the flat."

Mix went into the house and straight for the stairs, taking in the family pictures lining the walls on her way.

"Julia?" Dot's hands rested on her hips. "Jessie's filled me in on your little plan. What's going on?"

"I told you she never left the village."

Jessie looked around. "Where's Dad?"

The wooden doors of St. Peter's Church flung open, and a flash of blue stumbled down the stone steps. Georgia charged out at a sprint. Inches behind her, red-faced and roaring, Clive snatched at her. Unlike on the stage, he caught her with thick fingers and yanked her back. Blood trickled down his face, and Clive's eyes went straight to them. They darted to the side, and Julia saw the approaching officers from the small army outside the station.

"Get *off* me!" Georgia screamed and thrashed, but Clive's thick arm only tightened around her neck, holding her tighter. As nimble as she was, she was tiny compared to Clive.

"Let go of the girl!" one of the officers screamed, approaching. "Clive, we know what you've done."

DI Christie hurried down, and Julia's heart skipped a beat when she saw Barker right behind him. He scanned the green and let out the same sigh of relief as she did. Julia's relief vanished at the sound of glass smashing. She looked at her café as Clive reached through a hole where the door window used to be and unclicked the lock.

"Stay back!" he cried, fumbling in his pocket. "I'm a man who has nothing to lose. You know I'll do it!"

Julia rushed across the green as Clive pulled a red cap off a metal bottle. He doused himself and Georgia in the lighter fluid he'd lit the campfire with. Georgia yelped, all of her bravado gone. He splashed the rest around the cafe before throwing the empty can into the corner. His lighter came out next, and he held it in the air, pushing a gasp from the growing crowd of onlookers assembling behind the wall of officers blocking the main road. Julia stopped by the edge, feeling Barker's fingers slipping through hers.

In the middle of her graffiti-ruined cafe, all Julia could see were the eyes of a terrified child.

"Mum?" Jessie whispered behind her. "Keep him talking."

"What?"

"Just do it."

Jessie slipped past Dot and Percy and walked back towards the cottage.

"Was any of this worth it, Clive?" Julia called, switching her gaze. "Did you really need the money that badly?"

"Oh, you have no idea." He grinned, tightening his

grip. "Jett could have been on the gravy train with me. All he had to do was sign! The record labels were all lined up and ready to go. You know how many chances artists get at his age? They wanted those songs."

"But let me guess, the record labels weren't so interested when you tried to replace him and carry on like nothing had happened?"

"Julia..." DI Christie warned. "The negotiators are on the way."

"But that's what happened, Detective." Julia looked to the church. "This whole thing has been about Clive Winston making as much money from Electric Fury as possible, and Jett Fury was the only person standing in his way." She turned back to the café. "That's why you brought your little puppet Jax to the village. He didn't want Tia's place, did he? You made that up."

"Very clever." Clive flipped off the cap of the lighter. "Something poor Jax can't claim to be. He's been going along with things for months."

"Months?"

"*I* was behind him leaving the band." Clive laughed. "The promise of fame and fortune was all it took to twist his ear. He was happy being Jett's footstool all those years. I had to make Jax really hate him. Make him think he could be the front man. Once it was in his head, he wouldn't stop hounding Jett. I knew Jett would flip and fire him."

"Jett was special!" Georgia cried, making a fresh attempt to struggle away. "Jax couldn't even pretend."

"They're *all* pretending!" Clive roared, yanking her back. "Jett fed off the crowd too much. I needed someone who could understand that this is a *business*. He was too driven by ego. He didn't care about the money, he just wanted them to love him."

"Isn't love all anyone wants, Clive?" Julia called. "You were married once."

"To a putrid witch."

"Enough reason to give up on people?" Julia stepped forward, tugging free of Barker's grip. "You've had a whole life to figure out that money only goes so far. Jett was cruel in his own ways, but he cared about more than the numbers."

"The whole world revolves around money!" Clive backed into the counter. "If everyone had just done as I said, none of this would have happened. Jett could have had it all."

"What have you got, Clive?"

He snarled and held the lighter higher.

"I bet you regret it now." She took another step forward. "Faced with prison or death, you have nothing to look back on. Nobody around to notice when you're not doing well, nobody to steer you, nobody to forgive you."

"People cause problems. I just wanted an easy life."

"*You* caused your problems. You orchestrated this whole thing and were too blind to see how it could fail. You didn't even consider that a fancy dress wig wouldn't be made from human hair. You made all of this so much harder for yourself than it needed to be." Julia relished seeing the flush of his cheeks. "Let Georgia go. Georgia wants those things. She wants a family and has her whole life ahead to find one. If you're going to burn down my cafe and take yourself with it, leave her out of this. She's done nothing to you. The police had figured it out before Georgia invaded the stage."

She glanced at Christie, and he scratched his neck at Julia's assumption.

"Why do you care so much about her?" Clive's grip tightened, and he flicked on the lighter. "You'll lose everything whether or not she dies. She's nothing to you."

Julia's mouth curled into a smile, but her brows furrowed.

"I wouldn't lose everything." She looked back at her family. "Once upon a time, it would have been the end of my world. It was my sunshine when I needed

AGATHA FROST

it. I could have stayed there, soaking up that slice of sweetness forever, but I learned that there's more to life than what you do to make a living. It's too late for you either way, Clive. And you know it. If you want to burn my cafe to the ground, do it. It's just a building. I'll pull up a chair, get out the marshmallows, and start planning for the next one."

"It would kill you."

"You can't kill me that easily." Julia held out her arms. "Just let her go. She's a child. She's still got a chance."

Clive grunted and lunged forward. He flicked the lighter and the flame lit up the graffiti. The crowd gasped, and Julia felt Barker move in closer behind her. His grip tightened around her hand as a shadow hovered through the beaded curtain.

Keep him talking.

"Why the rehearsal at the church?" Julia called. "That's the one thing I couldn't figure out. Did Jett really ask you to move the rehearsal space? From what I could tell, he wasn't all that bothered about going to the rehearsal in the first place, and those echoes didn't sound all too pleasing to my ears."

Clive's smirk confirmed his lie.

Julia had only heard the information about Jett wanting to change from Clive and Mix. She shouldn't have assumed Jett was the one to tell Mix. A simple

292

question that could have ended things during her first conversation with Mix.

"Go on," she said. "This was *your* big plan. What was the point?"

"The press, flower!" He laughed. "You think they'd care about a washed-up rockstar's death? I needed to give them something *electrifying* to fill those column inches and finally get Electric Fury some headlines. I thought about doing it on stage to really get people talking, but a dash of mystery and a hint of intrigue goes a long way to creating a legend. You know he *refused* to do interviews too? He owed me this much after making my job so difficult for so long."

The drone hovered behind him.

"And it *worked*! Finally got everyone talking about a nothing band like Electric Fury." His smirk stretched wider. "But I should have known Mix would get the bigger headlines. I should had kidnapped her a long time—"

The drone nosedived at the lighter.

Julia held her breath as it spiralled towards the soaked ground.

It landed on its base, and the lid shut itself.

In the confusion, Georgia bit down into Clive's hand and kicked the lighter away. He growled in pain, yanking her back by the hair. Officers crept in, but another tug back on Georgia halted them at the door.

Georgia let out a pained whine through clenched teeth.

Behind Julia, Jessie grunted as she sent the drone diving at Clive's face. The corner struck his eyebrow, causing him to cry out and swat. The drone wobbled, settled, and dove in a loop to his other side. He howled as it collided with his cheek. As he stumbled, Clive snatched at the drone, but finally catching it meant he loosened his grip on Georgia. She kicked backwards, landing a boot on his groin, and wriggled free. Georgia sprinted through the door, leaving Clive half-hunched as the officers closed in around him.

Georgia ran straight past Evelyn and Shilpa and into Kieran's open arms behind them. Julia smiled, glad he hadn't given up on her just yet.

"How did you figure it out?" Christie asked as his officers dragged the man away kicking and screaming.

"Aside from the fact he's been acting like a self-interested pig this whole time?" She held up her palms. "His hands, Detective. Right before Jett was electrocuted, Clive shook my hand, and his hands was as dry as sandpaper. I didn't know it at the time, but they were covered in the glue he'd poured all over the fuse box. I didn't make the connection until my gran did the same thing while fixing her drone."

"The *glue*?" Christie sighed. "You figured it out from the damn glue?"

"I should have known from the premature celebration that same night. He wasn't celebrating because he thought Jett was about to sign, he was celebrating because his plan was about to go off without a hitch. I just don't think he counted on how much Jax had over-egged his pudding."

In the calm hallway of her gran's cottage, Julia rested her head against the wall and let out a sigh of relief.

"You saved the day," Jessie said. "Forget the café, you should work in hostage negotiation."

"*You* saved the day," she said, accepting her hug. "Nice flying. You were right about why he chose the rehearsal at the church. Kinda cool."

"And *I* told you that drone would come in handy!" Dot jerked a thumb into the sitting room. "What *is* she doing?"

In the mirror above the mantelpiece, Mix was applying bright red lipstick. She'd changed into pleated navy trousers, a white blouse, and a navy blazer.

"Your gran let me raid her wardrobe." Mix dragged black sunglasses from her hair. "With or without?"

"For your police interview?"

"For the pictures."

The sunglasses went on before she slicked back her blonde hair, still wet. She checked her teeth for lipstick before stepping away and assessing the outfit from the back.

"Julia!" Dot cried from the front door. "The circus is back in town."

Hoping her gran meant the literal one, Julia pulled back the net curtains as several vans screeched to a halt across the village green. She pulled away as men with cameras rushed out.

"Your grandmother has quite the selection of newspapers in her bathroom, and boy, did they have a lot to say about me." Mix fluffed up her hair and back-combed sections with her fingers. "Did I ever mention that Jett wrote 'Lightning in a Bottle' the night we met? Ten minutes with his guitar and he wrote the band's biggest hit. He was right, I am lightning, but the lid has gone and I'm ready to burst out of that bottle he's kept me in all these years." She turned to Julia and held out her hands. "So, how do I look for my walk to the station?"

"Did you tip them off?" asked Jessie, leaning in the doorway. "Nice to meet you, by the way."

"The famous daughter." Mix glanced over her glasses and looked Jessie up and down. "Don't suppose you play any instruments?"

"Sorry."

"Shame." Mix pushed up the glasses, checked the mirror one last time, and walked to the door with a swagger Julia hadn't seen from her before. "And yes, I did tip them off this time. I hope I see Clive before they send him away to rot so that I can thank him for setting all of this up. He's just made me the most famous woman in the country for the next fifteen minutes. It would be silly to let this opportunity go to waste, don't you think?"

Mix strutted down the hallway towards the open door and the flashing started in an instant. Julia pulled her gran back from the blinding bulbs as Mix sauntered towards the gate with her head down. They swallowed her up in a circle as she walked towards the police station, their shouted questions going unanswered.

"Why don't I look like that in those clothes?" Dot grumbled almost to herself.

"You do to me, my love," said Percy.

"Thank you, dear, but I have eyes. Julia, I can't believe you found her in a van less than an hour ago. What is she doing?"

"I think she's fed up waiting to get everything she ever wanted." Holding onto the door, Julia looked out to her cafe. Even in this state, she couldn't help but smile, pulling Jessie into a sideways hug as Barker joined them from behind. "Time to go home."

None of them seemed to want to get out of the car outside the cottage. Exhaling into the silence, Julia let the weight lift.

"It's over," she said, resting her hand on Barker's. "Thanks for a wonderful date night."

"You two are sick." Jessie laughed. "C'mon. Looks like they're having fun in there."

Julia looked to the cottage where her sister was cheering at something one of the children had done. It looked like Katie and Vinnie had joined too. Resting her eyes, hand still on Barker's, she let the silence sit for a moment longer.

"You were wonderful tonight." Barker's voice brought her back. "It's on record that you told Christie about the newspaper message."

"I couldn't prove it without Mix." Julia un-clicked the seatbelt. "All's well that ends well, though, I suppose. Except for Clive and Jax."

"Man with green hair can't be hard to find." Barker opened his door but leaned back and said, "And it's not all well for John, either. He *chose* not to take your report any further. He also missed the van on several searches of the forest. You'll never guess which aristocratic family the superintendent married into."

"Does it begin with Astley and end with Smythe?"

"Bingo. I wouldn't put money on him being this village's resident detective for much longer. I feel bad for the guy, but given how he's been acting since the divorce, I can't help thinking he brought it on himself."

Barker climbed out, and Julia followed. She looked off to the soft glow of the cottages dotted across the dark night and wondered if John was having the worst night of his life somewhere out there. She didn't wish tough times on anyone, especially not one of Barker's friends, no matter how he'd been acting lately.

Still, as Clive and Jax had shown, it was difficult to stop the sparks from spreading once the desperation switch had been flicked.

She hoped he'd be alright.

In the end.

But for tonight, she'd done all she could.

She turned to her cottage and let Olivia's giggles brighten her smile as they pulled her in.

25

"I can't help but feel a little responsible," Brian said a week later, on Julia's forty-first birthday. She'd met him in his antique barn. "We only met a few times, now that I think about it, but when you get to my age, seeing anyone from the old days feels like a family reunion. I went to that big house he said he still owned, and it was flattened and turned into houses years ago. I hope the pig rots behind bars for what he did. Anyway, I thought this could go in the café once it's finished. Happy birthday."

"You can't blame yourself." She kissed him on the cheek. "Thanks, Dad. I love it."

Carrying the antique brass scales further up Mulberry Lane as the first brown leaves swirled around the cobbles, she stopped at Katie's Salon for the 'special birthday treatment' she'd been insisting Julia have all week. She had to wait for nearly an hour owing to her packed-out waiting area. When the treatment eventually started, Julia wondered what she'd done in a past life to deserve such torture.

"*Ouch*, Katie!" Julia yanked away, trying to ignore the giggles coming from the other customers. "Is it supposed to hurt this much?"

"Don't be a baby," Katie muttered through the threading string clenched between her teeth. "I'm almost done. Just a couple more hairs and – *perfect*! What do you think?"

Julia stared into the mirror and held her breath to stop the gasp that wanted to burst out. She wriggled her brows, hoping to lower them, but she wasn't arching them.

"Erm…" Julia wriggled the thin lines where her eyebrows used to be. "They look exactly like yours."

"Great, aren't they? Okay, time for your top lip."

"Oh, no, thank you."

Katie forced her back into the chair.

"Julia, it wasn't a question."

After another ten minutes of whimpering at the agony of having her skin pinched, Julia returned to her quiet cottage and headed straight for the freezer. She pressed a bag of carrots across her mouth.

"Sounds like Mummy's home," Barker said as he carried Olivia in. "Are you having a good birthday so – Julia, what happened to your eyebrows?"

"Katie's latest qualification happened."

Called to the dining room by Mowgli's scratching claws, she opened the door, so startled she dropped the bag of carrots inches from the cat as he shot out of the room.

"*Surprise!*" cried her whole family, minus Katie. "Happy birthday!"

"You always make your own birthday cake, so we all chipped in and tried our best." Dot rushed over and snapped a party hat onto her head. "Katie got you too, then?"

Looking around the room, Julia was relieved that she hadn't been the only one subjected to Katie's latest qualification. Jessie, Sue, and her father all sported a similar look of frozen shock and awe.

"Now, what do you think?" Dot asked, pushing the seven-layer rainbow cake as it tilted dangerously to the left. "I don't know how you get them to stand upright, but I'm sure it tastes fine. I made the pink layer." She thrust a knife into her hand and whispered, "Stay away from the green layer if you don't want to be eating shells. Your father cracks eggs like he's never seen one before."

Julia had expected to return to a quiet day at home

with Barker and Olivia, but she was just as pleased to spend it with her family. They played party games, picked at the buffet, and as had become the case with most family functions these days, the kids became the stars of the show. Once everyone started to filter out by late afternoon, Julia asked her gran to hang back.

"Birthdays can be a clean slate," she started, "kind of like the start of a new year, and I've been thinking—"

"You can spare me your schpiel, dear." Dot lifted a hand. "I've already made the call. We were discussing the future of the group at that meeting you interrupted with your 'paradise' revelation, and we all decided it would be best for Peridale's Ears to go on an indefinite hiatus. With Johnny being so hectic with wedding planning and the paper, and everyone else being so busy or old, I don't have the energy to keep rallying the troops when they don't want to be rallied. Percy and I will continue to keep an eye on the village, of course, but no more meetings for the time being. I know I get a little..." She paused to clear her throat. "Carried away, sometimes."

"You, Gran?" Julia smiled. "Never."

"I'll let that slide because it's your birthday." Dot headed to the front door, where Percy was waiting for her. "Oh, and Julia? Try to not look so surprised."

"I don't think that will be possible for a while."

Julia joined Barker in the kitchen, where he was still picking at the buffet spread out across the breakfast bar. He pulled a paper folder from the top of the fridge and handed it over. It had a small red bow that immediately sprung off as she opened it.

"Every single person who vandalised your café," he said as she flicked through the social media profile screenshots. At the same time, Mowgli swatted the bow around the kitchen. "Pulled all of their faces from the doorbell camera on my office door, and since everyone puts their entire lives online these days, they were easy to track down."

"Have you taken these to the station yet?"

"I thought you'd want to do the honours."

"You did an amazing job finding them all." Julia stamped the bin pedal and forced the folder onto the used paper plates and cups. "But I'm happy to move on."

"I can't say I'm not a little disappointed," he said as he pulled a velvet box from his back pocket. "Maybe you'll like this more. It's from Olivia."

Julia snapped open the box to a delicate bracelet. She pulled it out, and all four of their names were engraved on the inside of the band. Julia loved it so much that she wasted no time putting it on.

"They will grow back, won't they?" she asked Jessie on their walk down to the café later that afternoon.

"Or are we permanently stuck like this for the rest of our lives?"

"As long as we stay away from Katie's threading string, we'll be fine."

They reached the village, and though it wasn't as calm as it could be, Julia was happy to hear the clanking of the builder's tools coming from her café. Not that she could see it behind the parked tour bus blocking the view. The black covering had been ripped from the windows, and the inside had been painted bright white.

"Ah, there you are." Mix hopped off the bus. "I heard you were having a birthday party, and I didn't want to crash, but I also didn't want to head off without saying goodbye."

"You'd have been more than welcome. Where's the first stop?"

"London," she said, exhaling a shaky breath. "Time to strike while the iron is hot and the press is fresh. Already got a few meetings with labels lined up, so yeah...thanks, Clive!"

"Have you heard from him?"

Mix shook her head. "And I never hope to. I visited Jax. He's not doing great, but after he admitted he was the one who ripped off the tape and poured the water on Clive's instruction, he's looking at a good few years behind bars."

"After what he did to you, it's the least he deserves," said Jessie.

"Are you sure you can't play any instruments? You've got the look, kid. You'd be perfect in our band."

"Not a single one. And I'm tone deaf."

"*Our* band?" Julia asked.

"Tia on the drums, me on guitar and vocals, and ah, looks like she's ready." Mix waved up the street, and Julia followed her gaze to the B&B where Georgia and Kieran were sitting on their bags on the pavement. "Kieran's going to be our new official roadie. Turns out Georgia is quite the show-woman and has a half-decent voice to match. Takes after her father in that regard, for all his faults."

"Are you sure that's wise?" Julia asked.

"No." Mix laughed. "But, she reminds me a lot of myself at that age. Granted, I never did *half* of what she's done, but she just needs guidance. I'm probably not the right person to do it, but Tia's level-headed enough for the three of us. Like me being trapped in that recording booth for days, having to face the idea of her fiery death straightened Georgia out. She's accepted that Jett is dead, and she's promised no more shenanigans. I've had enough time to think about how I'd have run Electric Fury, and now it's my time to see."

"You're continuing the band?"

"I'm not *that* crazy." Mix laughed again. "We're starting fresh. New songs, new name. Tia suggested 'In The Mix' with me as the frontwoman, but we'll see. Who knows, you might hear us on the radio one day."

"I really do hope so." Julia held out her arms, and Mix awkwardly went in for a hug. "Just look after yourself, okay?"

"I'll try. I think we're going to look after each other. Us lost women need to stick together. If we start off on the right, *fair* foot, what can go wrong?"

Tia came from the direction of Jessie's flat, where they'd been staying, carrying only her own bag this time. She tossed it on board with a nod and a raised hand. Julia thought that was all she would get, but Tia gave Julia a quick squeeze and a peck on the cheek.

"I hope you know how lucky you are," she said to Jessie. "See-ya."

"I think we should be off," Mix said, looking around the village. "I was tempted to stay for a minute, but I don't think I'm yet done chasing my dreams. I have some awful parents to prove wrong about what I'm capable of. I can't go another year proving them right."

"No hope at reconciliation?"

"The second they heard I was alive, it was back to the usual. When they started listing the conditions of how I could be 'allowed' back into the family, which, yes, did include me marrying one of my many second and third cousins, I put the phone down. I don't need their conditional love. I've never felt a shred of warmth from them in my whole existence. I'm living life my way from here on out."

"The best way to be," Jessie said, shaking Mix's hand. "Good luck."

"Are you sure you don't want to come?" Mix asked, stepping back onto the bottom step. "You can learn instruments. It might be an adventure."

Jessie took a moment to think about it.

"Plenty of adventure waiting for me right here," she said, wrapping her arm around Julia. "I'm done with life on the road, for now. But go and have enough fun for the both of us."

"We'll try. Any last parting words of advice?"

"One day at a time," Julia said, glad to see Mix smiling. "But you already know that one. How about this? Flow like water and always look for the positive."

"Flow like water, I'll take it." Mix dug around in a bag on the counter. "And Julia, since you did enough for me, here's how I can repay you. A little goes a long way."

Mix tossed something at Julia before closing the door. They'd ripped down the barrier wall to the front cabin, leaving her to jump behind the wheel. Honking the horn, she pulled away from the café as Julia twirled an eyebrow pencil between her fingers. Laughing to herself, she looked on as Evelyn hugged Kieran and Georgia before they hopped onto the bus.

"Glad to see the back of them, Mum?"

"Oh, absolutely."

"Excuse me, love," one of the builders called from inside the café, nothing more than an empty box of freshly plastered walls and wide-open possibilities. "The police dropped something off around the back not long ago, and it's blocking the back door."

Intrigued, Julia and Jessie walked down the alley and into the café yard.

The popcorn machine stood where it had on the one day of the festival she'd got any use from it, though it was in even worse condition than when she'd first seen it in her dad's shop. The glass had been smashed, the kettle twisted out of shape, the plug and wire were missing, and judging by the algae and caked-on mud, it had spent the last few weeks living in a river.

"The famous popcorn machine," said Jessie, giving it a pat. "What are you going to do with it?"

"I've got just the place for it. Help me lift it."

They tossed it straight into the yellow skip atop a pile of Electric Fury memorabilia sitting in a box sporting the post office logo.

"Now." Julia dusted off her hands and opened the back door. "Should we figure out what our new café will look like?"

Thank you for reading, and don't forget to
RATE/REVIEW!

The Peridale Cafe story continues in...

**MARSHMALLOWS AND MEMORIES
Coming October 25th 2022**

Join Julia for another cosy adventure featuring scenes from Jessie's perspective for the first time!

You can pre-order the eBook on Amazon now!

Thank you for reading!

DON'T FORGET TO RATE AND REVIEW ON AMAZON

Reviews are more important than ever, so show your support for the series by rating and reviewing the book on Amazon! Reviews are **CRUCIAL** for the longevity of any series, and they're the best way to let authors know you want more! They help us reach more people! I appreciate any feedback, no matter how long or short. It's a great way of letting other cozy mystery fans know what you thought about the book.

Being an independent author means this is my livelihood, and *every review* really does make a **huge difference.** Reviews are the best way to support me so I can continue doing what I love, which is bringing you, the readers, more fun cozy adventures!

WANT TO BE KEPT UP TO DATE WITH AGATHA FROST RELEASES? *SIGN UP THE FREE NEWSLETTER!*

www.AgathaFrost.com

You can also follow **Agatha Frost** across social media. Search 'Agatha Frost' on:

Facebook
Twitter
Goodreads
Instagram

ALSO BY AGATHA FROST

Other

Printed in Great Britain
by Amazon